ON THE EDGE OF INSANITY

By

Valerie Smith

 New Generation Publishing

Introduction

As a child of probably three or maybe five years I would sit at the top of the lane hoping that my 'real' parents would come and pick me up and take me to my 'real' home! I would not accept that the parents I had were really mine. They never showed me any love or attention, nor did they care for me. All I knew was paedophilia; even at three I knew it was wrong and I vowed to myself that I would take my so called parents and my brothers and sisters away from such an evil place. Whilst I was young I did not consider my father as a perpetrator, I wanted to also protect him I guess from himself. I took responsibility for all living under my roof and would ensure they all ate well. I was last to eat; they would come first. Probably that's why I suffered from malnutrition and asthma. Whenever I had to endure a sexual ordeal with my father, from giving him pleasure at three years old to sex at eight, or being molested by my uncle or my next door neighbour, or when I'd catch my father having sex with the next door neighbour's wife (when I was encouraged to take part), it somehow made me more determined and I knew that I would one day overcome the effects and turn a negative into a massive positive.

I was a very quiet child, a very slow developer; I could not read until I was about nine, although I was good at maths. School was my cut-off; I could lose myself in learning, but would dread 3:00pm as it meant going back to the noise of a large family fighting and the bullying, especially from my elder sister, who was incredibly jealous of me. I think it was because my father showed me favouritism.

At eleven the sexual abuse stopped from all quarters and by the time I reached fourteen I found my life more relaxed. I could form relationships with people my own age and did not rely on the family as much. I started going out to youth clubs and being very creative with a needle and thread, finding I could make unique fashionable outfits which were admired by all my peers. This made me feel good and I became the centre of attention, something I had never experienced in my life before.

GCSEs came. I did not do very well and with no encouragement from my parents to further my education I became employed as a receptionist in the local hotel. I stayed for a couple of years then moved away from home to Bournemouth, where I worked for a further two years. I then moved to London, still working as a receptionist in various hotels until I saw an advert in *Hotel* magazine for a receptionist needed in Bermuda. No language barrier! I applied and was offered the job. It took about three months to arrange and so I managed to save and buy some summer clothes in that time. I had never flown before and I met up with a couple of girls who were also going to work in the same hotel, the biggest and newest on the island. I was excited and enjoyed the flight, and could not believe the sight of the island as we approached landing.

Being summer it was very humid and hot but very, very beautiful, a total change from what I had experienced back in England. Life was good. I managed to save and also spent spare time in America on holiday. BUT, I knew this was not for life. I had to go back home one day and confront the fears that were lurking inside me. I did not know just how badly I was *damaged* by my past at that time, but subconsciously it was eating away at me.

Chapter One

Until my mental illness surfaced I was in denial. Growing up, I could remember the abuse from my uncle and next door neighbour, but not the sexual abuse from my father. It was not until I became what I would consider mentally ill that I knew something was wrong with my family and the way they interacted. I started to analyse each relationship I had with my parents (my father died when I was thirty) and my brothers and sisters.

Excluding one brother, the way we communicated was far from normal. There was an undercurrent. The past was not to be spoken about. So when I disclosed to them that Dad had abused me, my sisters did not show any compassion and my younger brother accused me of being treated by a psychiatrist who had planted seeds in my head. The remaining brother accepted what I had said and started to question his childhood, which, in my opinion, was the correct process. By doing this he helped both me and him. He gave me comfort, reassuring me that at least someone in the family believed me, which strengthened my relationship with him. During the course of my treatment I discovered other sinister events that had happened, and so my relationship with my brother became even more valuable.

My return from Bermuda after two years away from England found me twenty-two years old. I was at a loss as to what to do next. I stayed with my family for Christmas and then travelled to London to gain employment. It was there I met my first husband. We met in the early winter of 1974, and were married in June 1975. I accepted his proposal because he was the first person to ask me at the time and I thought he would provide me with a good standard of living when he eventually qualified as a chartered surveyor.

The marriage was doomed from the beginning. I accepted nothing but perfection, and he was far from it. I thought he was ambitious, but he did not seem to have the same aspirations as me. He made a hash of his exams and after four years taking and retaking his first exam he gave up. I had given him total support; I gave him time to study and when he did not achieve his goal I took that as a personal failure.

Financially, he did not come up to expectations and I had to further my career, now in sales support, to keep up our image, and with my creativity in finances we did just that, but all the time I was totally unhappy with the marriage and found other relationships to satisfy my needs. I enjoyed life, forever socialising after work with colleagues, drinking to excess and constantly looking for other conquests.

I do not think I knew what happiness was, so at the time I did not even know I was completely unhappy. The thought of leaving him did not come into my head but I was forever comparing him with friends who were successful and this made me feel jealous. Yet deep down I felt I did not deserve any better!

With my creativity we had managed to acquire a very large family home (2,500 square feet of property) and were mixing with wealthier people. I knew my husband was feeling totally inadequate and I was becoming more and more disillusioned with the marriage.

After eight years of marriage we started to try for a family. We tried for a year and then took advice from our GP. I had complications because I only had a period every four months, which made it very difficult to conceive. Having undergone tests it was established that I was not ovulating. I was put on Clomid and had to use fertility charts (having to take my temperature every morning). Given the stress of our relationship, of course conceiving was a problem! At the point of giving up, but with me still on Clomid, we were told by my GP to go and forget about trying for children and enjoy life if we could.

I was totally devastated. A family was crucial to me. I longed for children, I needed a family. I needed a child more than my marriage, although I had no intention of giving it up (my promiscuity had ended when I started trying for a family).

To my amazement the next month I found I was pregnant! Words do not convey my feeling! I was so elated, for a short time my husband and I were even happy. The pregnancy did not have any problems and although I had a terrible birth – **forceps and hands** – my daughter entered the world.

I was in total heaven! I was so proud to be a mum, and notwithstanding my childhood ordeals I became the perfect mother in every way.

I took to motherhood like a duck to water. I was totally wrapped up in caring for my daughter; she meant everything to me. She was a lively child, but enjoyed the quiet times with me alone. I made lots of friends who had children the same age and for the first eighteen months I was engrossed in bringing her up.

When she was eighteen months old we tried for another child. I was put on Clomid once more, conceived and then lost the baby at nine weeks. I was devastated. How do you mourn the loss of a child never to be held in your arms? Not only this but I was becoming conscious of the age difference I would have between my children and there was a delay before I was put on Clomid again. My GP was absolutely marvellous and fully supported me. He said he would arrange for me to go to Queen Charlotte's Hospital in

London but there was a nine month waiting list! I was emotionally drained and disillusioned with the whole proceedings. My friends had all had second children and I seemed unable to cope with seeing them with their families.

Nine months eventually passed and I went on my own to see the consultant. He was absolutely fantastic and even gave me his telephone number should I need to speak with him over the coming months. I was put on Clomid straight away and in six weeks I found out I was pregnant again. I had to go back to see the consultant for a scan and there was a risk that if he could not see a heartbeat he would have to arrange for me to have a D and C. To my delight, there, at six weeks was a heartbeat!!!

I was told to go home and book into my local hospital for maternity care. But the pregnancy dragged and I was worried all the time that something would go wrong. I had sugar diabetes in pregnancy and they would not let me go over my due date. I was admitted to hospital to be induced and was twenty-six hours in labour with a caesarean to follow! I woke up to the joys of being handed a little baby boy! I said immediately to my husband, 'Shall we have another one?' but he was not amused.

My family was complete and, although extremely tired from the operation, I somehow coped despite little help from my husband. He seemed to wrap himself in work, spending little time at home. The children reached six and three years and did not seem to care whether he was around; as long as they had me they didn't seem to worry at all. I became suspicious about the time my husband was spending away from home. He would go to work on a Monday, not reappear until late Wednesday evening, go again and then not return until late on Friday. I found a cassette of love songs in his car – completely out of character. When I confronted him he said it was a friend's. Then one weekend he said he was going away to think about the future and came back on Monday evening saying he wanted a separation. I asked if there was someone else. He denied it. I explained there would be no separation. Or divorce. Nothing.

The next week he left me. I did not take any action until the end of the week. A friend got me to phone a solicitor who lived close by. He came to the house and took some details. He said that from what I had told him, he was probably having an affair. I thought about it overnight and then started to phone round his friends. It seemed I was the last to know that he was having an affair with his boss's secretary. I was raging. I felt so alone. We had just moved to another county so I did not have a friend to call who lived nearby. His friends must have alerted him as he then called me. I said I was going to take him for every penny I could get and with that he said he would be home in two hours. It was at this point I started smoking again after eleven years! He returned and we went out for a meal. How I stopped myself from tipping the whole Boeuf Bourguignon over his head I shall never know! I wanted answers. He explained the entire sordid story to me and then agreed to try to start again. I was confused, but I could not accept that the marriage was over. I wanted it to work. I thought we could have a second chance.

Chapter Two

Starting again meant learning to trust him. He agreed not to stay away from home and for six months he stuck to it religiously. Sex improved for a couple of months, but then stopped. I was tussling with my emotions, still smoking, and drinking in the evenings. I had no one near by to discuss the situation with and the children noticed the change in me.

One evening I put the children in the bath, and went for some reason to sit in the snug. In the armchair, all of a sudden I heard the video talk to me! I was totally perplexed and for some reason forgot my surroundings and was completely engrossed in what it was saying. I was transfixed, glued to the chair. It said that I must stay with my husband if I loved him. I had no idea what love was, so I could not reason with it. The monologue must have lasted at least fifteen if not twenty minutes and I could hear in the background my children shouting and becoming frightened as I had left them alone so long. I snapped out of the trance when I heard the children running down the corridor (we lived in a bungalow). THIS WAS THE START OF MY ILLNESS.

I remember it was March. I knew I had no alternative but to end the hopeless situation. I knew I had to first get a job which would pay enough to cover the bills in this huge property and provide enough for a nanny. I had always wanted to go into sales, and as I was excellent with money I thought I would apply to become a Financial Advisor with a local company. At the interview I had to fill in a questionnaire and when it was marked the interviewer established that I was a HIGH FLYER and welcomed me with open arms. I had no idea what skills I had and was totally unaware of my potential. All I knew was that I had agreed to join the company and was handed files to digest, ready for an exam to be taken in two weeks, my passport to a two week training course in Swindon.

I went home numb. I knew I would get the job but I was anxious. Forgetting the huge hurdle I had to face, I immediately phoned my husband at work and told him I was taking the children out the next morning. He was to take his possessions and leave, pending a divorce and a financial settlement. I did not have time to miss him. The children totally accepted the explanation I gave them and carried on with their usual daily routine they were used to. My head was spinning; I had to arrange for a nanny and get her mobile. My first task was to get a bank loan for the nanny's car. My luck was in when I met the bank manager. He was leaving the bank that day, so he broke the rules slightly and agreed to give me a loan regardless of the fact that I had not had any experience in a sales position. He was impressed with the equity that was in the property so he knew one day I could repay the loan.

We had such a laugh in the meeting. He was showing me different body language poses, some quite risqué. The person in the next room complained about the noise we were making. At home later, he telephoned me to ask me out! I accepted and had a ball. Someone actually found me interesting. I had not been in that situation for a long time!

Studying was hard; I had not studied for so long. Responsibility for the children made it difficult. My husband started to call before the children went to bed in the evening, but they were not interested in talking to him, so that stopped. Naturally I told him what I was doing and I knew by the tone of his voice he was not impressed – memories of his days studying made him feel inadequate.

*   *   *

Prior to my marriage break-up, when my son was about two years old, I found myself changing his nappy one afternoon. I can remember this particular day like it was yesterday and it will always be in my mind until the day I die. I can recall looking at him lying on the changing mat quite innocently, and I had this burning desire to sexually abuse him! I do not know to this day what stopped me. These urges continued on other occasions when attending to his needs but at each time I managed to refrain from abusing him. During the course of my treatment, as I unearthed yet more sinister secrets about my siblings and parents, I became incredibly impressed with myself that at the time I had not harmed him. I can only assume that the marriage break-up happened at the right time, giving me other things to occupy myself with so the nanny cared for him more often than I did.

Chapter Three

I studied hard despite my concentration levels being very low. There seemed to be an undercurrent affecting my progress, as if my subconscious was pulling me back from achieving my goals. Part of me was very negative, but another part of me was very positive; it seemed there was a conflict going on within myself. At first, in between studying and the children I arranged to interview nannies. I had no idea how I was going to make ends meet, but I had no choice. I desperately wanted to keep the property but I had no idea whether I could. My first priority was to ensure that the children were happy with my choice of nanny.

Once in place and her salary agreed (with board and lodging and the use of a car, including at weekends), I had more freedom. As much as I loved the children I needed time away. Caring for them over the years, the problems conceiving, complications during labour, the break-up of my marriage while having no one to talk to and now studying for a career were having a destructive effect on my state of mind. Whilst I kept it together when dealing with the children, I was becoming more impatient, volatile and unable to relax. I was constantly worried about the future, my cash flow and my new career. The day came to take my exam and I was naturally very nervous. So much depended on my passing!

It was in the afternoon, a Friday. If I passed, then I would have to travel to Swindon the next Sunday to take another exam on Monday morning. Passing this would mean further exams each morning. If I failed any of them, I would be sent home. I took the exam, I remember there were about twenty questions. I managed to answer them all and when it was marked the trainer asked me to look at questions 18 and 20. I thought, was that all I had answered correctly? 'You only got two wrong!' I had passed! How could I so lack confidence? Somehow I had remembered all the course work and could pass exams, but physically taking them was putting an immense strain on me. No one to celebrate with, I got inebriated on a bottle of champagne.

Sunday came, I said my goodbyes to the children and nanny. I would ring them every night to wish them goodnight and to tell them I loved them dearly. It broke my heart to leave them, but at the same time I longed for a break from the responsibility I had. The training centre in Swindon was a well organised centre and in pleasant country surroundings. I had dinner that evening and met some of my colleagues on the same course. I was confident and excited about the coming week. Monday came and went, the exams were taken, which I passed, and I met a good bunch of people on the course. We relaxed in the evenings with a drink or two in the bar, but I knew that I was not able to enjoy the evening as I should. I had immense worries; I couldn't seem to focus fully on the course even though I passed all the exams. The following week was the same. I managed to pass all the exams and drove back home with enthusiasm and eagerness to start making money (I was self-employed) as whilst on the course I hadn't earned a penny.

Coming back from Swindon and entering a working office environment was difficult. I had been away from people for so long I was lacking confidence and felt completely out of place. Everyone seemed to have a partner and I missed going home to discuss the day with a husband, or partner; all I knew was those four walls. Selling financial products was not easy. People were quite hostile. Looking back I think my approach was wrong. I still had this conflict within myself plus the pressure to succeed!

Coping with the nanny and the children was a problem. One particular day I had just got into the office when an assistant from Tesco's rang me to say my nanny had just had an epileptic fit and an ambulance had taken her to hospital. Would I kindly arrange for someone to pick up my children from the store?! This was just one incident I could mention. Nanny number one had to go. She could no longer drive. Number two was a godsend. The children loved her. She was English, which helped, and was devoted to the children and she got them involved in her family too. I was much more relaxed with leaving the children with her and in the evening I had some adult conversation, which I had sorely missed in the past. She knew I was lonely and we talked about improving my relationship with the opposite sex.

One day I went for a glass of wine in the local pub and I bumped into a friend. He had this mysterious, aloof friend with him at the bar. We were introduced and, never missing a sales opportunity, I enquired about his finances and arranged to meet him in his home the next evening. His name was Graham.

Chapter Four

Graham lived in a bed-sit local to me and was twenty-two years old. Blond hair, blue eyes, slim and tall. When I entered his home I felt the atmosphere between us become electrifying. There was mutual attraction even though he was sixteen years younger than me. I found it difficult to keep on track with my questioning technique, but when I tried to close him he would come back with a retort that I in turn would overcome. We both were aware we had met our respective match, intellectually. The meeting came to a close and we knew that neither of us wanted it to end. He offered me a drink, I accepted and we gradually got to know a little about each other. It was Christmas in a couple of weeks and neither of us had a partner to take to our work parties, so we arranged to take each other. He asked me to come back to the flat later in the week for a meal. I was so pleased, to hell with the age gap, this was exactly what I wanted; somewhere to relax, talk and to have someone to start to enjoy my life with again.

Arrangements made, I went home elated and I could not wait to tell Sarah, the nanny I had become so close to.

The day came to go for the meal at Graham's. What to wear was a problem, I needed new clothes. Fortunately, going through a divorce had its benefits. I was quite slim, still being stressed. I went with Sarah to buy a new top and underwear. Jeans would be OK with my new attire. I told Sarah not to wait up for me! I arrived at Graham's and it was as if I was visiting my soul mate. I had never experienced such feelings before. Nothing else seemed to matter but meeting him, as long as my children were OK. When I arrived, the first thing he did was give me the biggest cuddle out. I had never been held like that before and I knew that he felt the same as me.

We talked non-stop, I established he was very close to his family, mum and brother. They both lived about thirty miles away. I talked about my marriage break-up, my children, but I did not have the same feelings for my mum and brothers and sister. At the time I was embarrassed about not having the same feelings about my family, but at that stage I did not know why. I felt uncomfortable about the fact that I lived in such a large bungalow and he in a bed sit. I, at that stage, did not know that he was in debt and looked upon me as a way out of his predicament, even though I knew he thought a lot about me. Late in the evening I got a taxi home and we planned to meet again at the weekend.

On the Saturday I arrived at about 1:00pm and I'd just had a difficult time with my ex-husband, trying to sort out a financial agreement. All he seemed to want was for me to take custody of the children. I learned through friends that his fiancée had no intention of looking after the children and she was quoted as saying that she would not give me a rest! My ex reluctantly took them for the weekend whilst I was at Graham's. He and I spent the day in bed just talking, smoking and drinking tea. I felt so relaxed and to talk to someone I was beginning to care about made me quite emotional. The weekend passed, Indian takeaway with champagne, and the rest of the champagne on Sunday morning with scrambled eggs.

Christmas came and Graham and I spent Christmas night together. New Year's Eve plans were made; we decided that we would spend the evening in a hotel away from others. Sarah babysat. It was there that Graham proposed to me and I accepted. We visited his mum and brother over New Year and they were delighted with the news and accepted my children and

17

the age difference. I wished Graham's mum was mine and I told her so. I felt I had finally found a family I was proud of.

Chapter Five

Divorce from my first husband became absolute sometime in December of the year we parted. Due to the incompetence of my solicitor the financial agreement was not finalised at the same time. When my ex found out about Graham he changed the settlement. I was falling into more and more debt, what with keeping the house going and paying the nanny each month. My sales performance did not meet my targets and I was therefore seriously thinking about selling the house, but house prices were falling. I thought getting married to Graham would help the situation as he would help pay the bills, but I had doubts about the marriage. When we were together I felt we could move mountains, but apart there was a nagging feeling, something inside telling me not to do it. This, plus the negative and positive conflict in my head, was making me feel more and more unstable. The run-up to the wedding, which was scheduled for late February with the honeymoon in Venice, seemed to be a test to see if one of us would pull out.

The arrangements for the wedding went ahead and because of the animosity within my family I did not invite my mum or elder sister. The men and my son arranged to wear top hat and tails and I, with the bridesmaids, wore black with scarlet trimmings! Most of us were blonde. We were striking. The reception was held at home, ideal as it had a large drawing room just right for the occasion and the day went off without a hitch. Venice was the most beautiful place I have ever visited and we had a fantastic time, but there was still a nagging feeling inside me that all was not well.

Arriving home, it was great to see Sarah and the children. But Graham had bad news in the mail. While we were away he had been made redundant. He had already moved in with me. I couldn't help thinking that I had yet another mouth to feed.

After getting my head around the situation I spoke to Graham, explaining my concern about finances. I suggested I put the house on the market as there was still a great deal of equity in it which could be put to buying another and paying my debts off. I also suggested that Sarah had to go and he would have to be house husband for a while, at least until he was in employment again. I also wanted to get another solicitor to finalise the settlement with my first husband. He did not seem to want to discuss the situation and was happy for me to make all the decisions, which was not what I had hoped for. I'd thought, aren't two heads better than one?

Getting back into work was hard, especially with all my problems at home. Graham seemed to enjoy not working and fell into looking after the children. They did not seem to mind being looked after by their stepdad.

The house was put on the market and a new solicitor found. I tried to help Graham find employment but he would get angry when I approached the situation. I was working every day, sometimes eleven hours. I was slowly becoming weaker mentally and as much as Graham was the first real love in my life, I started questioning his behaviour. It was as if he had a split personality; he would try to keep me under his control should I question his outlook on life or ascertain if he had any desire to work. It was as if he was waiting for an event that would give him financial rewards. I never left the subject alone, I would listen to his bizarre thoughts about life, and he used to say that if you waited long enough prosperity would come to you. I questioned this frequently because his theories did not seem to prove true. I believed that financial gain was achieved by hard work and tenacity. My new solicitor found it difficult to reach a settlement with my ex-husband – he said it was like dealing with a female! I was the male in the proceedings! The only solution was to get a barrister for a morning in court, which carried a £1,000 fee. The day of the court case came and I was completely stressed. But seeing my ex I felt reassured. He had the familiar stress rash on his neck and wrists and he looked terrible. It was obvious who made the decisions in his house and it was not him!

The court case came to an end, much to my relief. Graham was completely useless and I was embarrassed by the way he handled the situation. I was deeply regretting ever marrying him and I began to doubt his sanity.

The house was sold and we moved to a four-bedroomed house in a location about eleven miles away because property was cheaper and I had an office there. I thought this would be the turning point for us, but I was wrong. The relationship went from bad to worse and mentally I was struggling with the suspicion that Graham had control over me. This and the confliction of my own opinion of myself was becoming quite a strain.

January of the following year came around and I had to go to Swindon for a week's course in Business Finance. We were arguing the day I had to leave. Graham was becoming more of a recluse and I did not know what to do with him. I knew the children were suffering from not seeing me much and I was concerned about their wellbeing. How I managed to attend the course I shall never know but it was somehow a relief to get away and it was the last course of exams. I would then be fully qualified.

In Swindon I was the only female on the course and

I enjoyed the attention. The course I found very interesting, a breakthrough into business meant more money in commission. On the last day we had to role-play. There was a manager on the course and he watched with interest how my colleagues reacted in role-play. The trainer chose three men to go first and we had to score them; marks out of ten. The performances were very weak and they were marked three, four out of ten! Then the trainer said he could not discriminate between sexes and therefore asked me to come on stage. I do not know how or why, but I gave the performance of a lifetime and everyone agreed eleven out of ten! The manager in the audience said he wanted me to go to his office to present that same performance to his staff. When going back to my seat I heard a voice in my head saying 'THEY ARE NOT TALKING ABOUT YOU!' I knew then that I needed treatment but I did not know where to get it.

Travelling back home on the train (Graham had had the car) I was worried what I would find when I got home. Graham was completely different, the children were happy to see me, but it was not the happy home I had enjoyed in the past. I spent the weekend arguing with him about getting a job and by Tuesday morning Graham had packed his bags and was leaving. I was relieved, as I was devastated. I loved him so much and I knew by his actions he loved me too. We cried in each other's arms but we knew the relationship had to end.

I kept everything together, working the rest of the week and looking after the children. On Saturday an ex-girlfriend of Graham's came to see me. She had been in contact with him. He said that he wanted her to go to a gig in the local pub where he would be playing the drums. She asked me to join her. I wanted to see him, as I was concerned about him. I knew he was not mentally stable although I did not tell his ex. When we arrived at the gig he was so pleased to see me, and he gave me a cuddle. Then I established that there was a girl with him whom he wanted me to believe was his girlfriend. I knew that he was playing games; he wanted me to get upset – I was in the pub, Graham's wife, with an old girlfriend and his so-called new acquaintance! When I asked him what he was doing with three of us he suggested if I did not like it I knew what I had to do! Alarm bells were sounding and I knew he was trying to push me over the edge, so I left and went immediately home.

The next morning I went for a drive. I can recall it was a very misty January. I heard a voice in my head telling me to pull the car off the road, crash into the siding. It took all my strength not to do it. I drove to pick up the children from Sarah's parents', where they had stayed overnight.

I explained about the voice and Sarah was concerned. She did not know what to do for the best. The next day I had an appointment and I took the children with me. The appointment did not take long so I left them in the car. When I completed my business I thought I would be safe driving with the children, I would not hear the voice in my head telling me to crash the car, but I misjudged it and it took all my strength not to crash the car with us all in it! I knew then that Graham had somehow managed to take control of my thoughts and somehow was trying to cause harm to the children and me. I drove straight to my doctors', surgery where I got an appointment immediately with my GP. I collapsed when I got into his consulting room but he told me to go home and wait for a psychiatrist to contact me. I did not feed the children that day, all they ate was crisps!

I talked to Graham on the telephone. I said that I wanted to kill myself and that I could not cope with another marriage break-up. His reply? 'Do it.'

It was the next day when I was visited by the psychiatric team from the local hospital. A friend, a colleague, had come to see me, to my relief, as she was concerned about me. Together we arranged for Sarah to look after the children while I was taken to the psychiatric hospital for observation.

The Pink Room on the hospital psychiatric wing was where I was assessed, the colour meant to be soothing. I found it difficult to sit down and focus on the questions I was asked. They wanted to know about my family and the house I lived in. I could not understand why at the time. I was asked what time it was. I told them that my friend had a watch, she had come with me, and to ask her. She could not stop laughing. What type of question was that? I was not that delusional? I recall they asked me whether I wanted their help and I said 'Yes' at once. I knew I was not functioning properly.

Once assessed they advised me to stay for a week for observation. When I met the other patients, although inmates feels more appropriate a word, I relaxed and saw the funny side of things. The people in there seemed to be on the same wavelength and all I seemed to do was talk and smoke continuously. To be honest, I was relieved to be taken out of circulation and was looking forward to a rest. At times I looked anxiously at the doors into the ward; part of me wanted Graham to visit me but this also frightened me. I wondered if he knew I was in hospital.

It was not all pleasantries; I found the person next to me lying on her back on the floor dressed in a coat, woolly hat and sunglasses, knitting! One day when she heard me crying she brought me some Weetabix and tried to spoon-feed me!

The week passed and I was told I could go home.

They said the only thing wrong with me was that I had pushed myself too far and was like a typical doctor, under too much pressure. One of the psychiatric nurses said that I needed to get out more, and she said there was a doctors' party on the premises that evening and anyone was welcome. The children were still being looked after by Sarah's family so I decided to go. I had a drink at home first, for Dutch courage, and then got there at about eleven as I did not want to be the first there, being on my own.

I had a ball, I met the ear, nose and throat specialist and the hospital dentist. They both invited me to their flat to continue partying and we played on their Sonic computer game and gun. They were both fantastic to be with, they had pressurised jobs but knew how to relax. I got home at ten the next morning.

I discovered that whilst I was in hospital, the house had been burgled. All my jewellery had been stolen except a ring I had bought in Bermuda. They had also taken the children's Sega computer equipment. Sarah's mum had been taking care of the house for me and she said someone had been in the house other than the burglars.

I had taken Graham's house key from him when he left, but when she explained what items had been left around the house I knew it was him.

There had been a drumstick, an ornament of his and she had found a sodden handkerchief stuffed down the radiator which I recognised as one of Graham's. I was beginning to think that I was not the only one with psychiatric problems so I went to see Graham where he was staying with a friend.

He could not believe it when he saw me, he looked so shocked and guilty. I knew that he thought I had killed myself; I could see it from the expression on his face. He asked where I had been all week and I told him about the burglary. Graham said he knew about it, to which his friend replied, 'I thought you said you hadn't been to the house?' I knew then and there he was trying to cover something up. He must have seen the car in the garage and as no one was there, believed the worst, particularly after our last conversation.

I felt sick. I was totally out of my depth but at the same time I wanted to help him. I was concerned about his state of mind and confused about mine. Part of me wanted him back, but I was curious as to why he wanted me dead! I knew he would inherit the house if I died, but what about the children?

I grappled with my thoughts, but did not have the time to focus on them properly. I had to try to get back to some sort of normality. I needed to care for the children and get back to work. Fortunately this was made easier by Sarah's sister, who watched the children while I went out on my appointments. At least the bills were being paid.

Chapter Six

Graham was hardly off my mind. Whenever I was out I looked for him, when at home I wondered what he was doing. I spoke to his mum, which gave me comfort, and she had not taken sides so I could speak with her freely. His brother was a brick too and we did meet up to discuss the situation over a drink. Graham had been a twin but his mum had miscarried his brother or sister in the early part of her pregnancy. In the past when I spoke to Graham he said it was a brother, but how could he know? Many times he said that he would have made a brilliant team with his brother had he lived. My thinking on this was that I could replace his brother and we could become a brilliant team together, move mountains and become very successful. I could not work out why this did not happen.

Apart from work I had the children to consider, I was grieving and realised that the children had suffered too. One day while tidying my son's bedroom, I found he had put everything that reminded him of Graham under the bed and I realised that once or twice I had found him huddled under the bed with his treasures. He must have been seven years old. One particular day I took the children out to a local pub for drinks and crisps in the garden. My son came up to me with his crisps and said that the crisp packet had spoken to him. I sat him on my knee and cuddled him and we talked. I realised that he was far from well and needed psychiatric care. My son could not remember the time when his father lived with us and naturally he had become very attached to Graham.

I went to discuss this with my GP and he said he would make an appointment for the family to meet with a psychiatrist to assess us all. I was very concerned about my children and worried about what he would find. We all sat in one meeting and I explained what had happened in the past few years. I admitted my feelings of guilt about what I had put the children through. I blamed myself for all that had happened. The psychiatrist sat with the children alone. The next appointment was on my own with him. He said that my daughter was fine, although naturally worried about her mum. My son, on the other hand, like his mum, needed some further treatment. He was incredibly brave and would discuss his problems with me while walking to see the psychiatrist. I would divulge what he had told me as my little boy drew a picture on the blackboard; always of a PIG MAN!? The psychiatrist would then convey to him through me how to resolve his problems. This went on for about six visits, and gradually my son came to terms with his loss. During the next year he would curl up on my knee and we would cuddle whilst he cried his heart out to me.

My problems were much deeper. The psychiatrist got me to focus on the collapse of my second marriage. He did not give me much feedback except that I had married too soon after the first break up. I was still concerned about Graham's state of mind and talked about him a lot, explaining that when I last spoke to him he had said that he knew where I was going for treatment and that he would follow the psychiatrist around town! The only reason I felt Graham said this was because it was the way he could get closest to me. This was bizarre and the psychiatrist wrote Graham a letter to try to get him to see him, but Graham declined the offer.

Gradually my family tried to get on with their lives. I made plans to take them away in the summer holidays to a cottage with a swimming pool in the Yorkshire Dales. I took the ex-nanny Sarah to give me a break and also company at night. Apart from that holiday, I did not go anywhere in that whole year, all I did was work, contrary to what the psychiatrist had advised me to do the previous January.

I wasn't making a fortune, but I managed to pay the bills. I was solvent, which was an achievement since I did not get any help and I was looking after the children also. In the summer, my boss gave me an article about a book published by an American psychologist; its title was *Earning What You Are Worth*! I read with interest that it was a way of reducing your fears and succeeding in business to your full potential, and making your personal life more relaxing and pleasurable. I sent off for the book and it arrived in a few days. I could not put it down! It seemed to have all the answers as to why I was not reaching my potential. The book gave prescriptions to solve the psychological problems and I did not hesitate to start trying them out. Unfortunately for me I did not quite finish reading the book. At the end it had a warning that you should not administer the prescriptions if you had been sexually abused! Looking back I think that the warning should have been at the beginning of the book, but at the time I was still in denial as far as my father's sexual abuse was concerned, so would I have taken any notice?

The one prescription I recall, and which in my opinion caused the most harm, was the elastic band exercise. The book explained that whenever you got a negative thought you had to twang the elastic band placed around your wrist. At the time I did not know how badly my negative thoughts were affecting me, so the effects were very serious. I recall taking the children with Sarah to a local lake so that they could go for a cycle round it. It was twenty-six miles around so they would be away all day. Once leaving them and reversing the car out of the car park at the lake I heard voices in my head. I arrived home and became totally deranged! My mind somehow broke through my preoccupation and entered a world of optimism. It was like opening a dark room into bright lights. This only happened for split seconds then reverted back to reality. I then went upstairs, flung myself on the bed and swung my head ferociously around in a clockwise motion, then ferociously in an anticlockwise motion. I burst into tears and sobbed uncontrollably for hours.

I was terrified and thought I had really done some damage to myself. I somehow got control and managed to drive back to the lake on time to collect the children. I did not mention this episode to Sarah, as I was not sure exactly what was happening to me. I drove back home, cooked a meal and left the children to play while I took a bath. It was in the bath that I suffered uncontrollable laughter, lasting for about half an hour. In that time I forgot all my troubles. I remember talking to myself and telling the children that we had to stay in a local hotel for the night as Graham would be meeting us there the next morning. I drove to the hotel and booked us into a family room. We all slept well and the next morning we waited for Graham to appear. Of course he did not and so eventually we went home. It was there that I became deranged again. I went from having complete hysterics, doing a Michael Jackson style Moonwalk, landing on the settee saying I was Marilyn Monroe, breaking the legs off the furniture; to complete panic when I thought the house was going to be blown up! At that point I scooped the children up, and wearing no shoes I drove them to the local psychiatrist. In shock and unable to speak I had to write down on paper what I was feeling. The children were taken from me back to Sarah's and I was admitted for a second time into a psychiatric hospital.

It was there that I was again assessed and was then

put on chlorpromazine. I WAS SECTIONED FOR TWO WEEKS! I think this was when I was diagnosed as a schizophrenic, although no one told me then. My GP informed me at a later stage but only because I asked him what I was suffering with!

During my stay in hospital I used my time constructively. I never lost sight of my work and made appointments by phone for three weeks hence. I also made friends with a lady who was coming to terms with the loss of her husband and between us we helped each other, laughing a lot at each other's way of coping. We kept in touch for a while once discharged, but found it difficult sometimes to talk to each other by phone when we were trying to cope with our lives.

My mother came to stay once I was out of hospital to help with the children for a few weeks. It was then that I found someone to help more with the children. My new child-minder would pick them up from school and cook for us all. This helped me no end, but I was finding work extremely hard and I was not improving my sales so much as it was becoming more of a struggle to make ends meet. A psychiatric nurse would visit me, from what I can remember, once a fortnight. I don't think this helped me very much as I was constantly asking for sex abuse therapy. On one particular day he came to visit me, he cried on the settee! I had to administer to his emotional state, which was hardly helping me!

The sex abuse therapist, however, was incredible. Although the treatment was very harsh and I had to experience flashbacks on my own after her visits, she did manage, with time, to unlock my feelings and slowly the memories came flooding back to me. I was aware of what had happened but it was a number of years before I was totally convinced that my thoughts were real and that my father had on many occasions sexually abused me.

Coping with my emotions, working, administering to the children, it all got me down even further. I had no friends and spent time at home on my own. It was not until the following year I started to date! I saw a couple of people who wanted to take the relationship further, move in together, but I declined their offers. It was not until July of that year that I met a man named Daniel.

We met through work. He wanted help with his pension arrangements. He was a number of years older than me, which I found appealing, good looking, athletic, medium build and dark haired. Daniel had a daughter the same age as mine, so that was a bonus. He asked me out and I found myself accepting his invitation. We met at a local country pub and chatted all evening. He had travelled a lot, and to some places I had visited, so we had something in common, as well as, of course, our daughters. We agreed to meet again. During the course of our courtship I found him to be a very loyal person, both to me and to his friends, whom I had met on occasions in his local, and so the relationship blossomed. We spent most weekends together with the children at my home and for a while life seemed to be getting on track. I was at long last forgetting Graham, as I had not heard from him for a while, but was conscious that we were still married.

Chapter Seven

For some reason during the latter part of the year I stopped taking chlorpromazine and my mental health started to deteriorate. I found myself starting to think of Graham again, and spoke to my psychiatric nurse when he visited. I became preoccupied, and I recall having a conversation with Graham about time spent in Gloucester working as a car salesman at the weekend. He said that he was very good at this and made a considerable amount of money. He also said he had a relationship with a lady with two children. Gradually, piece-by-piece, I began to compare the relationships both I and this lady had with him. He was not sincere and I was becoming more aware of what kind of person he was. He did not have any compassion. He was ruthless and again I started to question his state of mind.

Telepathy: I understand this is possible between twins, but I'm sure it also existed in the relationship between Graham and me. With this and the snippets of information he had given me, plus his actions towards me when we broke up, and my intuition, I came to the conclusion he was a psychopath. He had used his techniques to try to get me to kill myself, or both myself and the children, so that he would inherit the house. AND from what he had conveyed to me, the lady in Gloucester had been treated the same way and had not been that lucky because I am convinced that she had killed her children (stabbed them to death). I believe she is in Gloucester mental institution for life for their murder, which was not her fault. I started to convey some of this to my nurse but because of my deterioration I could not explain it very well and it was at this point that he said I was to be sectioned again! I was given more medication to take and the day after I had to arrange with Social Services for the children to go to Yorkshire to their grandmother's.

Daniel was concerned; he had never seen me like this. He was very understanding and offered to take me to hospital. I was distraught, confused. I knew in my own mind what I had stumbled upon, but did not want to disclose it to anyone for the fear that they would think worse of me. Daniel got me settled in the hospital after I was assessed again and I was so pleased to have someone on the outside who cared about me and promised to visit me every night before going for his usual drink after work.

This time I was admitted for three weeks! I was very concerned about my state of mind and the effect another stay in hospital would have on my work. I was to sit an exam during that time for a new qualification required if I were to continue my job, but the night before the exam I was kept awake all night by a patient in the same ward and the staff would not let me go. My stay in hospital was not pleasant. At one point a very young psychiatrist assessed me and said he wanted to change my medication. I can remember he asked me what I thought about it. I thought his approach was very unprofessional and I said I had no idea what was best for me as I was not qualified in these matters. That particular night I went for my medication as usual and I mentioned to the nurse dispensing the drugs that my medication had been changed. The nurse said there had not been any change and was I refusing to take what was prescribed? I was confused and found the nurse to be very abrupt, her manner completely inappropriate and lacking in empathy with a patient suffering with mental illness. She seemed to be putting words in my mouth. If I refused to take my medication it would be noted on my records that I had not conformed. I refused my medication and was left with the thoughts that it was perhaps me that had not understood the psychiatrist. In my opinion, the nurse should have said she would look into the matter for me and would again ask me if I would like to take my medication.

The next day, in the corridor of the ward, I met the young psychiatrist and asked him about my medication. I think he did not expect a patient to approach him, and he was reluctant to talk to me. I was persistent and he did not seem able to cope with the situation. A psychiatric nurse had to come to his rescue. No one came to see if I was all right nor did they try to explain the situation further.

One day a few of the patients went to play volleyball. I had never played before, but was always eager to find ways to pass the time of day, so I took part. What happened, once I had got used to playing, I find difficult to explain. I remember I returned the ball with all my strength and so fast it passed the opposition and went completely out of court. I was so surprised and shocked by my achievement. That evening I felt invigorated and went to dinner feeling good. I was sitting with both male and female patients in the canteen and there were a couple of psychiatric nurses giving out dinner. All of a sudden I was overcome with a desire to go through the motions of being raped. I stood up and was overwhelmed by this urge and at the same time made the appropriate sounds, and this must have lasted for several seconds. The people in the restaurant became quiet, and there was a dead hush. Everybody was aware of what I was reliving, and all the females empathised with me. If any male had commented on what they had seen, I'm sure they would have been lynched by the females present. Again, I had no assistance from the staff to make sure I was all right.

It was a few days before Christmas and Daniel

35

wanted me to attend his Christmas dinner with the people from his work. I had already asked the psychiatric nurses if they could check with the psychiatrist to see if I was allowed to go. By the morning of the dinner I still had not been told of the psychiatrist's decision and I needed to arrange for someone to bring in my outfit! That morning I was assessed by a psychiatrist whom I had not met before. At the beginning of our consultation she said that I could go, but later she changed her mind. I am not sure whether she did this to see how I reacted, but I felt this was completely underhand. Because I was in sales and I was used to overcoming objections, I did not lose my temper and was able to discuss this amicably. To my surprise I could go! Surely this is not the way to handle a situation like this; a more suitable way could have been found to assess me.

The three weeks came to an end and I was allowed to leave the hospital. It was nearly Christmas, so Daniel drove all the way up to Yorkshire to get the children from their grandmother's so that they could spend Christmas with us. Christmas was very frugal, but being all together was really what mattered.

After Christmas I seemed to deteriorate further. I lost the will to carry on. There were meetings about changes in the work environment and I knew that I had not progressed after a stay in hospital; I went through the motions at work. I was worried about cash flow, but there was neither the concern nor commitment to succeed. I had come to expect the worst. All I knew was that I needed to rest, and for once the work came last. I made my excuses at work and spent most of the time in bed. Daniel at some stage moved in and although I made an effort at night to socialise the days were quite different. I took the children to school and once home went straight to bed until 3:00pm, when I collected them from school. I knew that I could not pay the bills so for a while I blocked this off. Spring arrived and somehow I found enough courage to confront the financial situation. I knew I had no alternative but to sell the property I lived in. What on earth I would be able to buy in the area was worrying. I had the property valued and then looked at what I could afford. I was totally despondent. The only type of property I could afford was a back-to-back terraced property in terrible condition. It was not until I went to a local building society and discussed mortgages that I established that although I was not working the lender would accept my maintenance award as an income and based on that I could afford a terraced house which had just been renovated by a developer. I was able to choose my décor and carpets. It was still a back-to-back house, and I felt sick at having to live in this type of house when I was used to so much better. The children did not seem to mind and once we had moved in the financial pressure was off my shoulders.

I began to pick up. I found that we could afford a holiday, so Daniel, his daughter and my family went to Malta for a week.

My relationship with Daniel developed and he suggested that I get a divorce from Graham. Out of the blue, Graham telephoned me and said it was two years from our separation and he wanted me to start divorce proceedings. As I was not working I was able to get legal aid and so the divorce went through in a matter of months.

Chapter Eight

Relations with Daniel were not brilliant. There seemed to be something missing. Not having a good relationship before with either my first husband or Graham made it difficult to ascertain what exactly was missing. Looking back, I was not in love with Daniel, nor he with me. It seemed to be mutual respect, but the sexual side of the relationship was OK. After a year or so of living with me, Daniel decided to change employment and much to my annoyance decided to take a job working from home. This proved to be unacceptable, as the only place we had for an office was the lounge downstairs. How could a family live in these circumstances? I began to resent the situation and the relationship between Daniel and I got worse and so I decided to end it. I asked him to leave. I know Daniel was upset about leaving me, but he knew I would not change my mind once it was made up.

When I looked back, I could see myself progressing and my confidence improving. I did not have a job, but I was managing with the maintenance payments and sickness benefit I received. The children were at this point coping with the change in their environment and together we progressed. I started to look for work and for a while I actually sold double-glazing. It was not too stressful and because I did not need a large salary, my life was harmonious for some time. I managed to save enough money to take my children to Euro Disney. We stayed at the best hotel on the complex and we all thoroughly enjoyed it.

In the summer of 1998 I decided to take my family and my niece camping in Bournemouth. I had to go to Horsham to collect my niece and at the same time visit my sister, brother-in-law and nephew. At that time my mind was questioning my sister's relationship with me. She did not seem to be sincere and on meeting her I found myself starting to analyse her every move. My nephew at that point was around four years old. Saturday evening my sister and her husband had plans to go out and they wanted me to look after their children. My sister explained that my nephew was not easy to put to bed. I said I would do my best. I did not know what to expect but I could not believe the look on his face. It was complete terror when I said I was going to take him to bed. He clung to the banister for dear life! I was determined to get him to bed and finally got him to his room. I put him to bed and gave him some comics to read. Complete relief now replaced the look of terror. I kissed him goodnight and all was well. It was not until the next evening that things started to slot into place. My sister took her son to bed and spent an hour up there with him. I found this unusual considering she had visitors, and when they offer you are more than grateful for someone else to put your children to bed. She finally came downstairs and started to wash her hands, saying he loved his *Beano*s! The penny dropped and I knew she was abusing her son!

What to do with that information was puzzling. How on earth could I stop this happening? Then my thoughts turned to the type of work she was doing. She was working as an Assistant Secretary in a private school for boys aged three and up. It was all fitting into place. I recalled that she said there was a teacher who had shown a fancy to her but – and what a but – he had been accused of molesting a child and had therefore committed suicide, so ashamed and disgraced was he! From the way my sister had explained the situation I believe it was in fact she who was molesting the children at school and he had found out about it. It festered in my mind for the rest of the summer and by the end of September I gave up work, I was becoming ill with worry. My finances were not too great either.

I had befriended a young girl in her late teens, Wendy, and she had partially started to live with us. This was a godsend as I was not functioning well mentally and she helped me with looking after the children. I knew I was deteriorating and all I kept thinking about was paedophilia. I wanted somehow to get my nephew away from my sister, but I had no proof. Who would listen to me? With extreme concern for my nephew I went with Wendy to the local police station and told them all I knew. They said to go home and someone would be in touch. I'm not sure how seriously they took me because of my record of mental illness.

The days that followed were serious. I became deranged again, started to have bizarre thoughts; something about a helicopter coming to land at a local leisure centre bringing my nephew and family to us, having got my sister arrested for paedophilia. At one point I even went with my daughter to pick them up. Of course, they did not appear. The whole family was worried about me, I was not sleeping and whatever medication I had been prescribed had long been discarded. The police did appear at one point but I could not speak to them coherently so I do not to this day know the outcome of my accusations. The days were a blur and I could no longer focus on my children's needs. Wendy and my daughter, being fifteen at the time, took over from me.

My condition worsened and one day I found myself getting into my car, which I loved – a Celica. I did not know where I was going. I drove first to my local shops to buy cigarettes and whilst stationary I threw my shoes out of the car. I then drove back to the large bungalow where I used to live, some eleven miles away, and parked the car on the drive. I then proceeded to open the door, walk casually into the snug and sit down, remembering the time I first became ill. A man appeared and I asked him for a gin and tonic! He asked me to leave and promptly I complied, conscious that I was barefoot.

I then drove to Milton Keynes, some twenty-five miles distance. I heard voices in my head which I was talking to, completely deranged. At one point I started to drive the car erratically, first accelerating then wildly braking. I was screaming at people in the street, not stopping at zebra crossings and driving completely out of control. I remember going round a roundabout, not giving way and ploughing into a car. I did not stop, and I had scraped down the side of the car; my lovely Celica was damaged. I did not care in the slightest, nor about the condition of the other car involved in the accident, or even if the people in the car were all right. I finally ended up in an office block with parking. There, I sat in the car for a while until a lady came out of one of the offices. I got out of the car and she offered me a cigarette. We smoked them and then I realised she was keeping me calm until the police arrived!

It was then that she disappeared and I was left with two policemen. They first breathalysed me and I know they thought I was on drugs. They took me to the local police station; paperwork completed I found myself locked in a cell. The time was about 3:00pm. I was left alone, not given anything to eat or drink, until I was put in an ambulance to be taken to a psychiatric hospital eleven miles from home. During my stay in the police station they tried at one point to get me to go home in a taxi, but I would not get into the car. It was then that the police officer twisted my arm up my back, called me a slag and pushed me into the cold, tiny cell, slamming the door shut. I was assessed by a police psychiatrist, but no one actually spoke to me. It was 3:00am the next day when I arrived at the hospital. I was taken into a lounge, where I met with the most attractive young male psychiatrist who was waiting to assess me. I saw that he had Camel cigarettes in his breast pocket, so I casually took the packet and proceeded to take out a cigarette, asking him for a light, which he promptly gave me. There was also a mug of coffee, obviously for him, but which, without asking, I drank!

I somehow thought this was a friendly chat; it was not until I saw three nurses, one male and two female, approaching that I knew I was in trouble! My personality changed, I became completely psychotic and my language was appalling. They took hold of me in the way they had been trained, lifted me off my feet and escorted me down a long corridor. I was struggling to get away, but it was impossible to get free!!

I was then forced into a padded cell, where they tried to give me tablets but I spat them out, all the time struggling to get free. They flung me to the floor face down, twisted my arm so that I would not struggle and jabbed a needle into my buttock! At that point they left me, locking me in the cell. I can remember I thought I was completely mad, my head was reeling and I was incredibly concerned about my mental state. With the effects of the medication I quickly passed out.

Chapter Nine

Unsure of how much time had passed I opened my eyes to see the door of the cell open. Once out I was assisted to the lounge where there were other patients and I was given something to eat and drink. Those early memories in the hospital were very hazy. I was in intensive care! I was worried and when I was told that I was sectioned for three months I was devastated. How would I pay the bills? How would my children survive without me? How would I be able to buy food for them? Did they even know where I was? Eventually the fog lifted from my mind and my normal thoughts started coming back. From what I understood, my sister in Horsham had been trying to establish where I was, but I told the nurses that under no circumstances did I want to speak to her. I feared for my life; I was not sure what she was capable of should she realise that I had been to the police.

The hospital psychiatric team were the best I had experienced. Instead of hiding what I was thinking in my delusional state, they encouraged me to talk about it. Not in great detail but they acknowledged my concerns, which made me feel more at ease with my thoughts. I was put on a new drug and most of the early days in intensive care I slept. I still smoked a great deal.

My daughter and Wendy came to visit me on occasions, brought me up to date with what was happening at home. I had to leave the finances to them and somehow they managed to hold off the creditors and have money to buy food. Cigarettes were a strain on the budget so to enable the family to eat I had to give them up. My daughter was also taking her mock GCSEs and I was conscious that I must be putting a great strain on her at a time when she needed all the support she could get. My son spent a lot time staying with friends, so at least some pressure was off my daughter and Wendy.

The days were long and I got few visitors. It was not until I was out of intensive care on one of the open wards that I got a visit from Daniel. I was so surprised as we had not spoken since our break-up. I gave him a big hug I was so grateful to see him. He took me out for a drink in the evening for an hour and this became a regular thing for the rest of my stay in hospital. We discussed my sister, whom he had met, which helped me to focus on the ordeal. In spite of my stay in hospital I never became despondent and was totally positive about the future although I was concerned about money and my children.

The days were long and I found it difficult to concentrate. I couldn't watch TV or read. I did not make any friends and I was lonely. How I managed to stop smoking I shall never know! Time passed and after about ten weeks they transferred me to my local psychiatric hospital where I was allowed to go home overnight to adjust to coming out after two more weeks. Christmas was looming and I had no money. Finally I went home for Christmas. I still had medication to take, which I made sure I took. Again Christmas was frugal but we were together.

For four months I stayed at home, worried sick about money. I was in debt to the tune of £9,000, a car repossessed, two children to feed and clothe, a mortgage, yet no job!

In May I saw an advert in the paper for an operative in a factory quite local to me, with hours of 5:00pm–12.00am. I knew I was not capable of using my brain, but I thought I might be able to do a manual job. The children said they could manage with being on their own and so I applied for the job and got it. I had never been in a factory before and did not know what to expect. The people were very nice and it felt good being out of the house again. My diligence led to the manager's asking if I could work full time through the day. I was beginning to pay some debts off and I accepted the job as I knew this would help me further in reducing what I still owed. It was also at that time when the government introduced Family Tax Credit. I found that because I was on low income I was entitled to additional benefit, which helped me even further.

Transport was provided for me, but eighteen months later, the factory did not want to use the agency I worked for. The manager of the factory wanted me to become employed by him, but I had no transport so I could not take him up on his offer. I was not yet in a sufficiently good financial position to buy a car. Whilst the people I worked with were very nice I did not really like working in a factory.

Because I was reliable I was on many occasions put on the molasses production. There were times when I was covered in the stuff and should the machines falter then the pressure was on me to get them up and running. Every day I had to walk through my town centre, not having a car, having been dropped off by the minibus, wearing hob-nailed boots, smelling of the factory and wearing no makeup. I had no one at home to support me or give me encouragement. No one to love, just responsibility to pay back my debts. It was at this point that I started to smoke again.

I began to look for alternative employment and the only vacancy I could find that did not stretch my mental capacity was working as a carer in homes for the elderly suffering with dementia. I had no idea whether I could manage to do this particular sort of work, but I did not have a choice. The salary was even lower than factory work, but there did not seem to be any alternative. I applied for a position in a local home, thirty minutes' walking distance from my house, and I got the position. I did not have anything to look forward to, I was very unhappy and the children were going through adolescence. I could not see life improving in the future. I was so preoccupied with the past, depressed and under pressure. I found it hard to live: I had gone from bad to worse. All my friends had been lost because of my mental illness so I had no one to go out with. All I had was work and coming home again.

Chapter Ten

Bringing up teenagers is a challenge for two parents; for one suffering with a mental illness it is practically impossible! My daughter was the most ideal daughter up until the age of eighteen years. It was then that she started to rebel, a reaction from all she had had to undertake during her life – tolerating a stepfather whom she did not like, coping with a mum who initially was too wrapped up in making money and running away from the past. She got affection from me on the run, but not quality time. From the age of fourteen, she did most of the housework each Saturday and also tried to support me emotionally when I was worried about finances. Because I was never given support by my parents I had to learn exactly what my daughter needed, often too late in the relevant stages. Communication suffered, of course, at such important stages, making it even more difficult to understand her needs. At eighteen she met a young man aged twenty-one and they started a relationship. Home life was intolerable; we argued a lot but somehow she had coped well with her O levels and A levels; however, she was unable to establish what she wanted to do in the future. University was suggested, but she declined the offer. She was at that stage working part time in a shop and continued this after leaving school. As life with me was getting worse, she moved into a bed-sit with her boyfriend. It was a gradual thing and, to be honest, I was too wrapped up in my own world, so I was unable to guide her through making this decision except to ensure that she was on the pill. She became wrapped up with her boyfriend's family, I suppose replacing me with them. She kept in contact with her brother, but hardly came to see me. I was very hurt by this and it upset me a great deal. I was at a loss as to what to do. I knew that her boyfriend was not working and from what my son said she was getting into debt because of it. Although I hardly saw her, I tried my utmost to be civil to her when I did and did not show my negative feelings towards her boyfriend. I knew if I did it would cause my daughter to become more hostile. Gradually, by setting an evening each week to go swimming together we found a way to begin overcoming our problems. I knew she was not happy and all I could do was give her support the best I could. On one occasion, I told her there was always a home for her if she ever wanted to come back.

Eventually, she started coming back home to visit more often until on one of these visits she burst into tears and said she wanted to return home! I was relieved and between us my son and I moved my daughter back home. I established that she was in debt to the tune of £5,000 and in addition she was emotionally drained. Gradually she started to pick herself up and during the next year or so she managed to pay back all her debts and had found full time employment in a local bank. We did manage to spend more quality time with each other, and the arguments for a while were not so frequent. We were both changing into more confident people and it was only natural to have conflict with each other.

My son's adolescence was quite different. He had had no guidance from a male role. He did not get on with Daniel very well and resented his moving into his home. He started to go off the rails at about thirteen. Although his respect for me never faltered he could not cope with his schoolwork. He never did his homework, and began to mix with the 'wrong type'! I was at a total loss, as at that stage in his life I was working night shifts in a care home and my daughter had to look after him. So many times my daughter had cared for him. When he was ill or scared in the night in earlier years he would go to his big sister for comfort! She never complained and between them there was a bond.

He started to smoke cigarettes and have girlfriends. At the age of fourteen, he and a friend a couple of years older than him decided to go joy riding! They took a car from a driveway and when manoeuvring it from the premises they knocked the owner's wall down. Then they drove it towards another town. Unfortunately for them the owner overtook them in another car, and did a handbrake turn to block the road off. The cars collided! The police were contacted by the owner and they came on the scene. My son decided to make a run for it and was spotted on a thermal imaging camera located in a police helicopter. A policeman with a police dog chased him and when cornered he was told to keep still, which he did, but unfortunately for him the dog still attacked him. The first thing I heard about this was at about 11pm when I was at home wondering where my son was. I had once again stopped smoking, but this tipped me over the edge and I had to submit to the dreaded tobacco!

My daughter and I went as requested by the police to the hospital and there we found my son having stitches administered to his leg where the dog had attacked him. I could not think of a suitable punishment for this episode, as grounding on previous occasions did not seem to help reform his character. He did not receive a police record as he was not of age.

GCSEs came and my son did not take them. His absence from school on numerous occasions over the past years meant that he had missed a lot of his lessons and he knew that he would have failed if he had taken them. He at that time was also being bullied at school, a situation which the school did not resolve. He was, however, very keen on cars and was interested in becoming a car technician. We found a suitable college where he took an exam for admission. He passed and enrolled for a two year course. His confidence increased and he became a much happier person. Being with tutors who interacted with him completely differently from those at school improved his whole outlook on life. However, during this time at college he got involved in the occasional brawl when out with his mates and came home with cuts and bruises on a number of occasions. Once his injuries involved a broken arm, which did not seem to deter him. It was at this point that he decided that he needed to go to anger management. One consultation seemed to help him and towards the end of his college years, his behaviour improved. In my opinion, at that time he mixed with the wrong type of person and the area we lived in did not improve matters either. He did have a relationship with a girl of the same age for about three years and spent most of his time at her flat. Again, I was unable to give advice, as I was wrapped up in work. The only advice I gave was that he should ensure that his girlfriend went on the pill.

On the bright side, my son did work, in addition to college, at the weekends in the same care home as I worked. He was employed as a kitchen assistant and also gave out teas to the elderly, which he did with compassion. I was particularly proud of the way he dealt with the residents, most suffering from dementia. He was very well liked and enjoyed the time spent there.

Once he was eighteen, my son and I had one-to-ones in the local pub on alternate Fridays as a form of bonding. We would discuss events that had happened over the years and current issues that may concern us. This helped us greatly, a mutual understanding of our problems was achieved, and the lager went down a treat!

Although I had to handle the problems on my own, and with a mental illness, I would have never missed this opportunity to help my children as much as I could. I learnt so much about them, myself and the way we had all been affected by our upbringing. Not only that, but it helped in the long term with how we communicated, with the arguments and with reconciliation.

Chapter Eleven

Daniel and I spent Saturday evenings together. He cooked, or I did, and the wine flowed too freely but it was a way of a release from the monotony. I had at that stage finally paid all my debts off and I was concentrating on paying the mortgage off and eventually saving so that if I became ill again and could not work then I would not be in such financial turmoil.

I was constantly worried about the past, the present and the future. I could not see a way of getting free from the effects of my childhood and gradually I was becoming more and more aware of the way I interacted with all men and even some women. I believe this was a turning point for me. I was beginning to analyse different types of people and the way I was affected by them, relating them to past acquaintances and family members – parents, brothers, sisters. It was a gradual process which seemed to stimulate my brain to recall events surrounding my anxiety and the initial findings I had made regarding my family. I then started to research events that had happened, consulting various family members. Gradually, doing this detective work, I began to put the jigsaw puzzle together piece by piece.

I had two brothers and two sisters. My younger sister I have already mentioned and I concluded she was a paedophile, living with her family in Horsham, working in a private school for young boys. My elder sister had always been extremely jealous of me. She had a son who sniffed glue and asphyxiated with the effects of the fumes. From a post mortem it was established that he had only done it the once. To this day I do not know why he did it. He was a very quiet boy, aged fifteen at the time of death. His mother and father were not happily married. They argued immensely, and were very physical towards each other when they had disagreements. I did not visit them frequently, as I was not very close to my sister, so it was difficult to ascertain what problems my nephew had. I know when he visited me as a child of five or six I was never allowed to put him to bed. His mum always did. Whether his death was an accident or not, I shall never know and even now, some twenty years on, I have not got over his death. I was incredibly fond of him.

My younger brother seems to be a recluse. To date he has never married and his only contact with the family is through our mother. I do not think he works, but seems to have money. He is incredibly fond of my mother, in my opinion too fond. He denies the fact that my father abused me, so I do not have contact with him at all. My elder brother, whom I have mentioned previously, is the only sibling who was not abused, in my opinion. The way we interact leaves me without doubt that he is capable of forming relationships and has three children with his wife.

This leaves my mother, the most difficult one to analyse. I believe she is a paedophile…

From my findings I think she abused my younger brother and my cousin who stayed with us when his mother, my mother's sister, was dying of cancer. In my cousin's late teens until he died in his early fifties when he passed away, he lived in a mental institution. Apparently he would visit mum on occasions whilst boarding at the institutions. During his stay with her he would try to get out of the window in the middle of the night. . He was completely deranged on those particular nights.

My children questioned my findings and often encouraged me to revisit my psychiatrist to check if I was still mentally stable. On one hand they were relieved that I was not becoming ill again, but on the other they were upset about the skeletons lurking in the family closet. It was at this time that the clinic changed my psychiatrist. My new consultant was Dr M Chawla and boy was I relieved! He had actually read my file, which unfortunately is quite a rare thing. Not only that but he showed a genuine interest in me and congratulated me on my efforts to overcome an illness. To my amazement he said that I had been misdiagnosed and that there was no way I was schizophrenic! I could have kissed him. He said that I was psychotic depressive in remission! To my relief I was comfortable discussing matters with him and he gave me the time in the appointments to do so. I'm sure on many occasions I overstayed my welcome, but he never seemed to have a problem with that. I was able to ask him all the unanswered questions I had that were making me anxious.

This was not an easy process though. I found it stressful because there was always a chance he could section me again, bearing in mind what I was saying. He showed me respect and listened with interest. This helped with my findings and gave me incentive to carry on. I recall going to the police station on two occasions to try to get them to investigate my younger sister's actions, but because I had a history of mental illness they did not take my accusations seriously. At first I was deeply concerned about my nephew and the little boys at the school, but Dr Chawla suggested that my mental health came first. If I was not well, then I would not be able to take matters further. At this time I was working at a home for schizophrenics. I found it very laid back. The progress in rehabilitation was very slow. I questioned the way the patients were looked after, which did not go down very well with the management.

My brain was improving day by day and I knew that I was now capable of going back into sales.

Whilst working at the home for schizophrenics I met a man who used to visit it on a regular basis to do the garden. He was a fire fighter, about 6'4" and a Scotsman. Angus. He was very talkative and would hold court when he sat and had a cuppa with the girls in the office. I was beginning to come out of my shell and found him a very funny man. He made me laugh a great deal, which made me realise how I had changed. I was much more relaxed in the company of men. About three months after I started at the home I happened to mention to him that I needed some work done at home in my garden. Living alone meant that I had to do everything, and as I was more affluent I thought I would get Angus to help me.

He said that he would come and see me that afternoon and I gave him my address and telephone number. The afternoon came round and Angus appeared. He priced up the work and I made him a mug of coffee and we chatted in the lounge. He was on duty at the fire station that evening so he did not have a lot of time but gradually the conversation came round to men friends. He knew that I used to go round to see Daniel on a Saturday evening on a very casual basis and we discussed that for a while, then he asked if I would consider having a relationship with him on a casual basis. He was married. I was quite shocked at hearing this but at the same time flattered to think that a man like him could be interested in me. I said that I wanted to think about this, as I had not looked upon him in that way. He told me that he had found me attractive from the time he was introduced to me and he looked forward to my answer.

That evening, whilst on my own, I thought about it and came to the conclusion that I wasn't getting any younger. What harm would there be in a casual affair? The fact that he was married did not seem to cause me any anxiety after all; my husband had never considered me! The very next morning Angus appeared, having finished his night shift. I was surprised to see him and he only stayed a few moments. He was worried that he had overstepped the mark the previous afternoon. I assured him that I was fine and did not mention the proposition and he left. I needed time to get used to the idea of our becoming lovers.

At that particular time I was changing a lot. I had bought a car outright, I was solvent and now I was becoming attractive to the opposite sex. I started looking at myself and I was gradually changing the way I dressed and my hairstyle. It had all somehow crept up on me. I also started thinking about the house I currently lived in and I was not happy living there. I had always wanted to live in the centre of town on a particular tree-lined avenue. One evening on night shift at the home it was all I could think about and I decided to put my house on the market. The very next day I phoned the estate agents and told them about my decision. With luck, they had a property completely renovated in that particular avenue. He told me the address and after work I went round to see the outside, as I could not view until the next day. I had arranged for my property to be valued and on the market the next day so everything was in order when I arrived home from work that day. I told the children and they were very excited. They knew how much I hated living in the area and so they were pleased for me.

I fell in love with the new house the moment I stepped over the threshold. It was as they said; completely renovated, all fully decorated in white, stripped pine doors, hessian carpets throughout apart from the ground floor, which was wood laminate. The kitchen and bathroom were to die for! I wanted to put an offer in for it immediately, but as I had not sold my own, the estate agent said to wait.

My property went on the market at 1pm. The same day I had three viewings and by 5pm I had two offers at the asking price; by the following lunchtime I had accepted an offer on my property and my offer for the town house had been accepted. I could not believe how lucky I was. I had the mortgage arranged within the next few days, and nothing could go wrong!

Chapter Twelve

The garden was not a priority now. The house needed sorting and I had no way of disposing of the rubbish that had accumulated over the past eleven years. Angus had a trailer, which he towed on his van, so I knew this would not be a problem. I saw him at work one day and explained the change of plan. He was only too pleased to help me and we arranged a morning for him to collect all the rubbish I had sorted out.

He was punctual, and between us we cleared the entire lot. We then sat in the kitchen with coffee. Making small talk for a while, I then picked up enough courage to ask him if he would like to go to bed. He did not need to be asked twice and chased me up the stairs to the bedroom. I was, much to my surprise, very shy and bashful. It was as if there was newness within me. My so-called confidence had disappeared. To my surprise I found he was the gentlest person I had ever been with. He never forced me to do anything I did not want to do. His concern was to ensure that he gave me pleasure and, believe me, he did. Embarrassed after the event we managed to plan another morning suitable for us to repeat the episode!

I had started to look at alternative employment. I knew I could do better than the type of work I was in. I started to learn computer skills, having bought a computer, and with my daughter's help I became more knowledgeable. I knew I wanted to go back into sales so I started to do some research.

Angus did not need any encouragement and he would come round to see me three or four times a week, on top of the time I spent with him at work. It was a gradual thing; I started becoming very close to him. I did not see Daniel at the weekends any more now I was with Angus. On one occasion that Angus came to see me, we were in the middle of making love when I started to get a flashback of a time when I was with my father. It came completely out of the blue, totally unexpected as I thought I was through with my flashbacks. I rushed to the toilet and went through the motions of being sick. It was the repulsion of a time when I had no control over my life, at three of four years old. After that I laid on the bed and my head felt like it had been cracked open. The pain was excruciating. Angus, used to dealing with someone in shock, wrapped me up and made me as comfortable as possible. He said I had three hours, and then I was to go to work. I suppose that was the way they were treated in the fire brigade when someone had had to face a crisis. I did go to work, but I should not have gone, as I was feeling unwell. It was at that point that I became totally convinced that my father had abused me and that I definitely was not in denial. The house move progressed, not without problems. I managed to resolve them and although it took five months before we moved in, it was worth it. Away from the back streets, into a better area, I could not believe the difference in me. The house did not need anything doing to it, apart from the addition of the odd piece of furniture. Angus was there to help on the day and all went smoothly.

He never seemed to be away. He called before a night shift and again at the end of his shift. I was becoming more and more attached. I knew I was falling in love with him. He had made it clear that he did not want to leave his wife, but I thought that I could persuade him as he never seemed to be away from my house.

He was making me feel like a real woman for once in my life. I had overcome the fear of a man and the past was not affecting me. Angus was initially a friend, now a lover and I wanted him forever. There were areas in my lovemaking that I had not conquered; the art of dressing up for a man for example. Angus had said that he had dreams about me, fantasies. He wanted me to wear black stockings and suspenders with my suit jacket that I had bought for interviews. One day on the spur of the moment I found myself driving to the nearest Ann Summers. I had never been in one of their shops, I had always been too frightened. I went into the shop and found myself comfortable, the assistants were so helpful. I bought the obvious, and a suspender belt and black stockings. A black bra would go with the outfit and black knickers, and my jacket which he wanted me to wear as he liked my brain! My plan was perfect. I knew he would be round to see me at 9am the next morning so I was up early, hair and make-up done and the new outfit on. I was so excited I could hardly wait. I found the whole preparation funny and at the same time sexy. The doorbell rang and I put a dressing gown over my attire in case it was someone else, the postman possibly. I do not know how I kept a straight face. He looked at my legs in the black stockings and stilettos. He grabbed my dressing gown and pulled it open and said 'It's not Christmas? Get upstairs!' It was so sensual to give a man such pleasure. Our lovemaking must have lasted three hours and I really did not want it to end. I believe that this was the end of my fear of men sexually. I was so proud of myself and I had a smile on my face for the rest of the day. Angus could not believe that I had wanted to do this for him and he was so pleased and thrilled that I had eventually come to terms with my problems.

Chapter Thirteen

It became more difficult to say goodbye to Angus. I was well and truly hooked, completely in love with him. I started to put pressure on Angus, I said that I wanted him to leave his wife. He refused, telling me that it would cause too many problems and heartaches.

It was at this particular time that my younger sister came to visit me with her family to see my new house. I had arranged a Sunday for them to visit and I had prepared a buffet lunch. I knew that I was going to glean more information from my sister about events at the school where she worked. I had invited Angus to come along for moral support, as I knew it would not be easy to talk to her.

They arrived punctually and I showed them around the house before we got settled in the garden. Angus arrived and I introduced him to my relatives. The day was going well until I announced that I had booked a holiday in Bermuda, going by myself. My sister, to my amazement, said that I should not be going. She did not give a reason but was totally shocked by the idea. I thought that she would have been pleased for me, but obviously she was not. Angus left early. It gave me the opportunity to question my sister. We went upstairs and I showed her my new wardrobe of clothes thinking she would be pleased for me. At that time she brought up the subject of the school where she worked. She mentioned the teacher who had killed himself, having been accused of molesting the little boys at school. I could not understand her bringing up this subject. Had she been a normal sister she would have thought that this would make me feel uncomfortable. I knew she was hiding something but I could not bring myself to approach her about what it was. They left late afternoon and I then sat and tried to work out what was puzzling me. Why did she not like the idea of my going to Bermuda? Why did she bring up the topic of the teacher again? Why did she not give me a big cuddle and say how glad she was that I was getting better and coming to terms with what had happened in my life? Being better myself I knew how normal people reacted and I knew then that my family was not normal, they were so negative and unapproachable. They never talked about our childhood. It was as if it had not happened and cuddles or telling anyone you loved them was taboo.

Chapter Fourteen

Angus was becoming sheepish. One day whilst visiting he told me that he would not be able to see me much as I was going to Bermuda and he was going to spend time with his wife on days away. He said it would be difficult to ring me in the evenings. It was at that point that my work colleagues found out about the relationship.

Apparently the staff were spreading rumours around the vicinity of work. I knew it would only be a matter of time before Angus' wife found out and I therefore wanted to warn him. I tried his home and spoke to his son, who told me he had gone abroad with his wife. I was furious! How could he have gone away without telling me? I was so angry and I wanted revenge! Apparently he was due back in a couple of days. I was seething. How could I get revenge? On that day he was due back I worked a morning shift and came home with a bottle of wine. I could not wait until the evening. I started to drink and soon found I had drunk practically the whole bottle. It was about 6:30pm and I picked up the phone. His wife answered. All I said was that I was the ADULTERESS!

She said she knew. She was incredibly calm and did not seem to have a problem with me, just Angus. I was so shocked by her manner. In about another half an hour I rang her again to ask if she was OK. She said she was fine and she had thrown Angus out! I thought how brave she was and I told her so.

That was the last time I had any contact with Angus or his family. I went to Bermuda sad, alone and totally unhappy. I really wanted Angus, but he had obviously made a decision not to see me again. I wrote him a long letter explaining my actions and delivered it to the fire station, but he never approached me again. Another great love in my life had ended in disaster.

The holiday in Bermuda turned out to be good. The island was just as beautiful, more affluent than ever. I quite enjoyed the time alone to reflect, and drink at the hotel bars. I met an Arab, a man in real estate and a pilot.

Coming home I knew I had changed even further. I was able to cope with men now and became even closer to women. I was able to make friends more easily, of either sex. Men found me more attractive and liked my approach to life and my positivity and sense of humour, which was coming out in me. The one thing I wanted more than anything was to be accepted in business, particularly with businessmen. I knew I wanted to go back into sales, probably become self-employed again. So I started to look into it. It was at this time I was having problems with my daughter. She was unable to cope with the changes in me and my findings about my family. She had again found an undesirable man and thought this would be a way out. Moving in with him seemed the solution to her problems. I was explaining all that had gone on in our family and the reasons why she found it so unbearable at home. This did not work and so as a last resort I wrote her a letter as follows:

My dearest daughter, I cannot apologise for my actions as it would imply I am not at the end of my recovery problems! You are seeing a mum grasp at the rest of her life embracing the future with tenacity and an immense newness. I want as any Mum would what is the very best for her children. I am not sure at this present time you are ready to move out and leave at such a crucial time the very family that fought for survival over the past years. I know I need you and your brother more than ever and together try and salvage what sanity we have and build an empire of love, respect, dignity and total adaptability to carry us through to a happy family unit with what resources we have!!

This did not have any impact, and again she left home!

Chapter Fifteen

The days dragged, I longed to pick up the phone and speak to Angus but I knew that if he wanted me he would make contact. My son was getting on with his life, both socially and at his place of work. The management and work colleagues were all very good to him and with a pleasing personality he seemed to get away with more than most. I, however, was trying to decide what to do with my dilemma. My younger sister was on my mind, and I was concerned about her reactions to the fact that I had gone back to Bermuda. I had discussed this with Dr Chawla, and had explained what she had said to me on my return from holiday, but, more importantly, it was the way she had pronounced the words, apparently it implied she wanted me dead! Initially I did not understand this, but Dr Chawla explained that what she was really implying was that she was concerned that I was getting better, becoming more mentally stable and would become more of a challenge to her. With this in mind it was only a matter of time before she would be found out. I decided to invite her family and our mother to lunch, again to try to establish what more I could glean from talking with them. I planned for this to be the last time I spoke with my younger sister, because I did not feel comfortable with her around me any more. I also decided not to tell her about Angus; it would be another feather in her cap if she found out.

Daniel and I had yet again started to see each other, and he was fully aware of what my intentions were. He came to see me the day before the lunch and being the kind of person he was, stayed over and helped me make lunch, giving me moral support, and poured me the largest gin and tonic before he left.

Having drunk the gin, I was ready for anything. My daughter and new man arrived; my son and his girlfriend were also present. I had changed so much from the last meeting; I was more composed, confident and I interacted with my children much better. My sister arrived with my mother sometime around midday. It was obvious to me that the undercurrent was still there; neither physical contact nor special greetings. I served lunch, which went down very well. We then went out into the garden with coffee and the rest of the wine. I did not control the conversation; I waited until my sister spoke. What I found strange was that my sister continued to wear sunglasses, as if she was hiding something. There was a silence and then she asked about Bermuda and whether I had taken many pictures. I said that I was not very good with a digital camera so I had bought a glossy booklet with all the spectacular views of the island. She was interested in which part of the island I had stayed in. I pointed out the area, and then corrected myself, as I had got confused; it was the area I lived in when I worked there. It was near Hamilton, St George's was the location. Completely out of the blue and out of context she said, 'I won't forget that name, that was the name of a lady that goes to our school that had an affair with the head teacher who has left now, but she still picks up her son from school.' I couldn't think why she mentioned her or the little boy. All I could think of was that the little boy, now probably somewhere between ten and eleven years old, was probably the boy that she abused when he was much younger, at the time one of the teachers committed suicide. I could not comment on what she was saying, all I did was make a mental note of it so that I could come up with the conclusion later. I think that she was trying to get me to discuss the happenings at her school to see how much I had worked out, but I did not make any comments.

Because we interacted quite differently, my mum watched with curiosity. She had not seen me for a year or so and was surprised at the way I approached my sister's comments and it was at that point she for once became quiet. There was a look on her face which made me feel uncomfortable, an expression I had seen before, long ago. To this day I am not sure in what circumstances or when I had seen that expression before, but I knew it was when I was in a vulnerable position. It was a feeling in me, as though she assumed that we were all abusers and it was normal to be like that! I felt a shiver down my spine, and I was glad I had broken free of this and my behaviour was normal. I said goodbye to them and I knew that this would be the last time I saw my sister socially.

Chapter Sixteen

Summer progressed into late autumn and with Daniel I took the family to the Algarve. Also with us on the trip were my daughter's boyfriend and a friend for my son to socialise with. The villa we stayed in was excellent and the weather good. This was my third trip to the Algarve, but I had no fond memories. I had spent the last two vacations there with my first husband.

It was whilst there this time that I decided to look into the possibilities of finding alternative employment. I knew that I was at the time ready to work in sales again. I had glanced at the *Sunday Mail* business section during the summer months and on my return to England I read the section in the latest edition. I rang the number on the Monday and details were to be sent to me in the post about a franchise will consultancy. I could not wait for the information. Having read the literature on arrival I was convinced that it was the type of business I wanted to get into. I discussed this with Daniel and he seemed to think that I was the ideal candidate for the job. Following a meeting with the Managing Director in Cheshire I decided to join his company as a franchise and attended a training course. There was a mixed bunch on the course from all walks of life, but I enjoyed it and did not have any negatives, albeit it was late in October and Christmas would be looming; cash flow would be tight but I was willing to chance it.

The training was good, but the guidance concerning marketing was weak. If I had done what was suggested, I would have gone out of business. I decided to start my own marketing, arranging exhibitions. I needed marketing pop-up banners, which I had made up with the guidance of the Managing Director. It was successful, but not enough for the luxuries in life like a new car.

It was not until I started exhibiting in shopping malls that my sales improved. I then decided to treat myself to a convertible – much more in line with the image I was trying to portray than the little hatchback I was used to. I was struggling with competing with men, but gradually getting more established within the company I had what I considered to be a great breakthrough in overcoming my ordeal of abuse. Women also affected me, but working with such a good bunch of women I also overcame these problems.

I worked throughout the first year and managed to pay the bills. My son was happy with his girlfriend and work, my daughter was still with her boyfriend, but I knew she was not happy.

One Sunday morning whilst working on an exhibition I received a call from my son's mobile, only to establish it was a policewoman at the end of the phone. She explained that my son had had a car accident and the fire and rescue team was cutting him from the car as we spoke. They did not know which hospital they would be airlifting him to, it was dependent on the extent of his injuries. I was in incredible shock; I was numb and had no one to talk to as I worked alone at these exhibitions. I packed up my stand and drove to my daughter's house. I explained what had happened and both my daughter and her boyfriend came home to wait for instructions from the police, so we knew which hospital to go to. Panic set in; was he going to die? What was the extent of the injuries? Why didn't I have a partner to help me through this?

After an hour the police rang and told us to go to Coventry University Hospital, which specialised in limb injuries. I did not know what to think, whether that was good or would he be in a wheelchair for the rest of his life? The drive to Coventry with my daughter and her boyfriend was terrible. They wanted me to put my foot down on the motorway, but I did not want to be responsible for an accident, I was in shock and felt so alone not having a friend to talk to.

Once at the hospital, we went straight to Accident and Emergency. In the private waiting room there were friends of my son; word had gone round and they were there to see him. As I was next of kin, I took priority over them when visiting. We waited a while before a male nurse came to inform me of his injuries. I did not understand the extent of his injuries, I just wanted to know that he would live, and walk again! I managed to establish that, and was taken to see him. He was drifting in and out of consciousness. At one point he came round and I explained he had had a car accident. He asked if he was in trouble. I simply told him that the person who had been in the car with him was not injured.

I could not stay with him; I was too stressed and worried. All I cared about was that he would live and walk again. I drove home still in shock and went straight to bed, having dropped my daughter and her boyfriend off at their home. The next morning I called my son's employer and did not explain his injures fully; my son explained at a later date the extent of his injuries. His right leg from the knee down to the ankle suffered various breaks and he had to have an operation to put a metal plate in his leg. His left knee had snapped the main ligament and needed an operation. He had a fractured skull and a torn ligament in his shoulder. No wonder I could not absorb all the injuries whilst in shock at the hospital. He would, however, walk again, but it would take about three months before he was able to put full weight on his legs. He would not work for

71

five months. I felt sick with worry, but still managed to work, although it was affecting my performance.

It was at this time I booked an appointment to take a will instruction with a man named Max Freeland. I had initially met him at a local DIY centre; he had approached my stand and asked to make an appointment with me. He made the appointment for himself, so I could only assume he was single. The appointment was for a Thursday evening and I recall I had to rush home after having visited my son in hospital.

Max lived about ten miles from me, and as usual I was prompt. He answered my knock at the door and he showed me into the lounge. As I suspected, he was alone, like me. He was of average build, about 5′9″, with a shaven head, blue eyes and a very pleasing personality; in other words lovely to talk to. I established whilst taking his will instructions he was separated (five years), had two boys in their twenties of whom he was very fond, one living on the same avenue as me! He was a sales executive and fifty years old. What more could you ask for?!

After completing his will I found myself talking to him for a little while. Not overstaying my welcome though, I left. I had not been home in half an hour when the phone rang, and guess who? The lovely Max! Apparently I had not written his address correctly on the receipt and so he wanted to check that things were still in order. I assured him that this did not form part of the instructions and when I saw him next with the will for signing, I would amend it. Then he said (nothing to do with wills), 'I wondered if you would like to go out for a drink one evening'. I was pleasantly surprised and said that it would be very nice. I could sense the change in his voice – he was pleased that I had accepted. It was agreed that we would go out that Saturday evening, no need to give addresses apart from the number of the house, as it was on his son's street. When we finished our conversation, I shrieked out loud and was really happy that he had called. I was excited at the prospect of going out with him and already I was thinking about what I could wear. My son had plenty of friends visiting him the weekend in question, so I would not be missed at the hospital.

The day came around to go out with Max. I had chosen on outfit which disguised my figure, as I was carrying a few pounds more than I would prefer. He was punctual, and I was met at the door by a wonderful smile. I could not remember the last time I was taken out; Angus had never taken me out, and with Daniel there had not been a date for years. We went to a local pub and found that we never stopped talking, there were no pregnant pauses. By the end of the evening, talking to him, I could not find a negative, although I did not tell him so. He was a delight to talk with and seemed to say exactly what I would want him to say in reply to my questions.

Chapter Seventeen

The next few weeks were fantastic. Max and I met once if not twice a week. There was no one at home; my son was still in hospital, recovering from his operations. I knew he would be out soon so I was making the best of my time with Max alone. Whatever Dr Chawla had done to me, I was for the first time holding down a relationship. It was as though my subconscious mind wanted to say the wrong things, but my conscious mind said the opposite to what I was thinking. It was a newness that had significant regard in this relationship with Max. One evening at home, Max came to visit. We had wine and listened to music. Towards the end of the evening the relationship got physical. Max wanted to make love to me, but after the relationship with Angus I was not going to be pushed into anything. I can remember giving him a lecture about not wanting to rush things, but towards the end of the evening I gave in!

I had never experienced lovemaking like that. Because I felt totally safe, wanted, needed, the experience was incredible! What had I been missing all my life? I did not realise until now just what love was all about. It was only two weeks from the time we met that we realised we loved each other, but lovemaking took a little longer, and boy was it worth it.

We planned a holiday in a cottage with a log fire for the Christmas that was looming; everything was perfect, I was in heaven. I did not know that I could make someone happy!

Sadly the bubble burst when my son came home. Obviously I was so happy to see him and he so positive about the accident, he was already planning his new car. Of course, his car had been written off in the accident. That was remarkable considering the extent of his injuries, but I was worried and anxious for his safety.

The relationship with Max did not falter, it grew from strength to strength. I was totally in love and I knew that he loved me the same. I met his family, his mother, brother and two sons. Everything was perfect. He wanted to know about my state of mind, he encouraged me to keep taking my medication, which Dr Chawla had prescribed. It was not until Christmas that my daughter experienced problems with her partner. He became violent towards her, and it was on a Sunday morning at 5:00am that Max and I brought her home. The police had been involved, my daughter upset and bruised she came back home. I was relieved. I knew she could do better.

That meant the house was full. I was happy that the family was safe from harm. Max took it in his stride; he was used to coping with people, either in the sales environment or in coaching boys from the ages of eight to fourteen in playing football. I loved him even more to see how he made people comfortable. My children felt at ease with him, and they could see how so very happy he made me feel.

The following year just got better. Although my children, who were now 25 and 21, found it difficult living with adults, we managed to cope with each other's needs. I stayed at Max's at the weekend and once in the week. My business improved and I could not be any more happy than I was. Max and I had had weekends away, and a visit to Italy in September. Everything was perfect.

My daughter, after the break-up of her relationship, was naturally upset, and to make matters worse she could see how happy I was. Thank goodness, I was at last able to console her and I knew from the bottom of my heart that it was only a matter of time before she met the man of her dreams. When she became despondent during the first few weeks back at home, I used to cuddle her, something that I could not have done since she was small. To my surprise she allowed me to. This was a breakthrough; we had come a long way to enable us to do this.

It was one night in January that my daughter was on the internet on a social network. This was all new to me, but my daughter seemed to enjoy the time spent contacting people of all walks of life. This particular evening she came downstairs and said that she had been in contact with an RAF senior aircraftman, a weapons technician who was based in Afghanistan! She was brimming with excitement and wanted to tell me all about him. I listened with interest and was so pleased that she had found someone more in keeping with her status. The days progressed, and she was not to be seen; after having dinner she went to her room and was on the computer for hours each evening. I was so glad that she was at last finding happiness from such a man. When she used to come up for air on occasion in the evening she said that they had so many similarities and views. She felt that they had been brought up the same way and that they could not wait to meet each other. Time passed, he occasionally telephoned her and they planned to meet in the March after he had completed his stretch in Afghanistan. The day finally came! My daughter had planned the day, what to wear, what to say. I wanted to be here at home at the meeting as a precaution, which my daughter accepted. He arrived! A charming man, with presents for everyone. I was impressed with his attitude and like Max was a gentleman. What can I say? He fitted in with the family and to date they have not looked back. They have discussed marriage, a family and all is going to plan.

Just another reason to move on, forget the past, draw a line under it.

Chapter Eighteen

2008! I have been in therapy for nineteen years!

Dr Chawla was very happy with me, I was able to hold a relationship down with the lovely Max, cope with work, and my efforts to relate to my family were paying off. I was so happy to finally have a normal life, something I had never been able to cope with before. I was emotionally sound.

Spring came, and Max and I went to Northumberland. We stayed in an hotel for three nights. We visited the local sites. I was relaxed, Max and I were still as happy and in love. Dare I think of the future? I knew that this was the longest time I had been with someone, still in love and happy. Boy, did I have a lot to thank Dr Chawla for! My whole outlook on life had changed! Before my therapy I had felt life was like a race, I would not appreciate my life in the present and enjoy my achievements to date, but put pressure on myself, looking at the mountain I still had to climb, never content with my life.

My daughter was still happy with the airman Charlie. He came to stay every weekend. I did not spend much time with them, but I knew she was still happy, all was going well.

My son, well, he had broken up with his girlfriend and was, I think, enjoying life being single, going out most nights. Again I spent even less time with him, but with him being a male, I did not have a lot in common with him. He worked hard and as far as I could see he was OK. It was hard to relate to him. Should I have spent more time with them?

Summer came and Max and I had a family wedding to go to. It was his son's wedding and a very lavish affair. I bought a very expensive outfit, and an outfit for the next day as accommodation was provided. I felt good, looked good and was happy to be with Max. I was made welcome at the occasion and danced the night away with Max. Could things get any better? After the wedding, Max and I drove to Hastings for a few days. I had just had a good month at work, so I could treat myself to a break. I knew when I got back home, I would cry; this was a common occurrence, when things were going well, I cried, which meant I cried most days.

Christmas came round quickly, all seemed fine in my household, Max wanted to go to Spain for the holidays. I thought it was a great idea, my daughter and Charlie were going to his parents for hols and my son said he would spend time with friends. So it was organised. Spain was good, weather quite warm, people friendly, plenty of English people there too. We hired a car and saw the area, again relaxed and at peace with the world. I didn't want to come home, I enjoyed it so much.

Chapter Nineteen

The next year was quite different. I had somehow kept my eye off the ball when it came to work. I didn't realise how difficult it was to keep my head above water. Cash flow was a problem, and in the last couple of years I had taken out a couple of loans to keep me ticking over. They were crippling me; I found it was difficult to keep up the payments. Marketing was another issue, it was becoming too expensive compared with the sales I got from it. This year I must look at an alternative. I had relied on exhibition stands, but interest was not as productive as I would have liked. I spoke to a work colleague, who had similar problems. She suggested door to door marketing. No costs involved. We designed a script, and then got started. Results were not too bad, but it took a lot of time each day. The economy was not too good, and that was also having an impact. Working for yourself is not easy. I was beginning to get worried, and this had a further impact on my business. I didn't tell Max. There were also marketing meetings I should have attended, but I couldn't face them. I was not keeping up with changes in the industry!

I didn't realise at the time, but my health was affected by all the worries I had that year. I managed to keep it from him, but Max must have noticed my anxiety; we were still seeing each other as usual twice a week. We didn't go away much that year as I wanted to try to turn things round. But, the year was slipping away, and Max suggested a break in Egypt, a cruise down the Nile. I didn't dare draw money from my account, so I asked Max if he could loan me the money and I would pay him back monthly. He agreed thinking that this was just a blip in my cash flow!

I neglected myself, I did not get any new clothes to go in, or get my hair done for the holiday. I didn't feel well, I found it hard to relax, alcohol was the only way I could relax. I was so worried about my financial situation. The holiday? Well I hated it. I had never been on a cruise before. At meal times you had to sit with six other holidaymakers – this was for every meal, this was annoying, I could not talk to Max privately, which I had always enjoyed on previous holidays. We also had to get up at 5am to go on the excursions as it was so hot later in the day. Problems with work back home, and now a holiday that I did not enjoy made me feel worse. The holiday came to an end! I did not feel refreshed as I had done after previous holidays, it was back home to my problems.

I started work again, found the complex wills hard to grasp. They were piling up, I found it hard to get back to the clients for signatures. I felt ill. I was still taking my olanzapine, but my sleep patterns were worsening. I was still seeing Max, but we were not as close. Then the bank manager called me. He explained that I was drawing more money each month than I was earning. My overdraft was reaching the level of my arranged borrowing! To combat this I had to agree to deposit £500 per week from my business earnings. I knew this was impossible, but I needed time to think. I was upset, I was supposed to go door knocking that evening, but I couldn't. Instead I got ready to go to Max's early; I knew I had to tell him my concerns about work. As I pulled up at Max's I thought maybe Max could help with my financial embarrassment? As soon as I saw him I started crying. He let me in, held me and then over a cup of tea I told him about my problems. Without me asking him to help, he got his cheque book out and wrote a cheque out for £500. He said that he would give me a cheque for the same amount each week until I had got back on my feet. I was so grateful, I hugged and kissed him but I knew that the days of my being a will consultant were numbered.

For the next few weeks I managed to get out of bed somehow, but my sales were down, I just could not cope any more. My daughter had announced that Charlie had asked her to marry him. I found it hard to get excited about it, all I saw was more expense as surely they would expect me to pay for some of the celebrations. My son had started a relationship with a young lady, whom I had met once or twice in passing. I did not have any friends to talk to about my problems, I was all alone apart from Max. He kept to his word, the cheques came regularly!

One day in autumn I decided enough was enough, I could not cope any more. I decided that work was to come to an end. I was going to put my house on the market, my son would have to get a flat, my daughter would have to stay with friends until the wedding, and me, well, would Max have me? I plucked up courage to call him. He was surprised, said he would like to discuss my decisions face to face, but yes there was no question, he would be happy to have me move in!

Chapter 20

I telephoned the estate agents, whilst smoking a cigarette – yes, I had started smoking again. They were happy to come out and value the property. Tomorrow would be good. I then telephoned the benefit office, but I was due a pittance as I had been self-employed. Coffee and cigarettes were going down well, but I was so stressed. I knew I had to tell the family, and it would be a shock to them.

The house was a mess, I had neglected it. My family had done little to keep it clean and tidy. I was so stressed I knew I couldn't clean it before the next day. So I went and bought a bottle of red wine, took it to bed with the cigarettes!

Tomorrow came, the estate agent arrived. He was impressed with the property and valued it at £150,000. With paying my debts off and mortgage I would be left with £60,000. Not enough to start again, but it would do as a nest egg for my retirement. He did, however, suggest I tidy the place up. When he left I set off cleaning the property, I had had a new lease of life. That evening I would talk to the family to discuss my plans.

The evening came, my son seemed happy with the news, but my daughter had concerns. Where would she get married from? This made me feel sad, unhappy it was not what I had planned for my daughter's wedding. I just said, 'Let's keep positive'.

I kept seeing Max, twice weekly and I tried to hide from him the fact that I was smoking. We seemed to still keep our relationship together. He asked with interest whether anyone had come to view the property and was concerned about what I managed to do to keep myself busy through the day as I no longer worked. I lied! How could I tell him that I just laid in bed, drinking and smoking, worrying, not eating, the house a mess?

No viewers. The estate agents said that it was the economy, would I think of reducing the price? I discussed this with Max and we said we would leave it for a couple of months till the end of the year.

I was desperate, I could not cope any more. Each day I drank and smoked! Friday the thirteenth of November came round. I woke early, had about six cigarettes first thing. At 7:55am, I dressed and went to the local shop. I knew at 8am I was allowed to buy alcohol. I bought forty cigarettes and four large cans of Fosters lager! I took them home, lined the cans up on the dining room table, and then got my olanzapine from my bedroom. There were twenty-one tablets. Between smoking, I drank the lager and took all twenty-one tablets. After consuming all the tablets and lagers, I went to bed and fell asleep.........

The next thing I knew I was on a hospital trolley being wheeled into hospital by two paramedics. I was constantly being sick, drifting from consciousness to unconsciousness. Apparently there was a queue for Accident and Emergency. Finally I got into an assessment cubicle. I remember seeing a nurse who did not treat me with sympathy. Again I drifted into unconsciousness. After a while, the nurse said that my daughter was outside. Reality dawned! I realised what I had done. I wanted to see her; so the nurse went to fetch her. But she had not come alone! Not only did she come into the cubicle, but in walked my son and MAX! I was ashamed, I hid my face with a sick bowl! My son checked that I was OK, then left. (He was the one who had found me and called an ambulance.) There was a conversation between the nurse and my family about whether I should go home, but Max had said that I was not in a fit state to go home as I was constantly being sick, and my emotional state should be checked. Eventually a bed was found for me. I must have passed out again as the next thing I heard was the sound of the wheels of a hospital bed being glided into a ward. I was relieved, I knew I needed help.

Once I was settled on the ward, Max and my daughter started to plan what they should do once I was given permission to go home. My daughter said my bed was not in a fit state to sleep in, Max said that he had no problem with my staying with him. I couldn't have cared less, all I wanted was to sleep. Eventually, we were called to an office where I met a counsellor or a psychiatric nurse, I can't remember how she introduced herself. When she asked why I had attempted suicide, Max and my daughter started talking about the past events. I could see and I told the nurse that this was exactly why I had attempted suicide, they were both against me, and neither seemed to consider the anxiety, worries I was going through trying to sort out a sale of my home and the impact it would have on my family. I was under stress, and needed support. Eventually, the nurse agreed that I could go home with Max and a counsellor would see me the next day at Max's.

I had a good night's sleep and breakfasted on toast and marmalade. Then I had a shower! I'd not showered the previous evening; with the sickness, I was in need of a shower. Afterwards I sat listening to music, trying to focus on the previous day's events. Lunch came – soup and a roll – Max was being very attentive. Neither of us discussed why I had tried to take my life. The counsellor arrived in the afternoon. She said I seemed a lot better, more focused. She said that the medication I normally took should not be taken until the beginning of next week, to have a break from it due to the overdose. The counsellor was very understanding, she could see that Max and I were very close, and did not question me about why I had tried to take my life. The rest of the day, I relaxed, spoke to my daughter, explained that a councillor would visit me at home tomorrow, so Max would take me home the next day. My daughter had plans, a wedding exhibition; so Charlie agreed to look after me. I went to bed early. How did I feel? Relieved. At least Max and my family knew what I was going through. I was worried about the future.

Morning came, Max took me home. Boy was I desperate for a cigarette! I saw the condition of my bedroom, the carpet stained with vomit. How was I going to get out of this mess? The house needed a good clean, but why should I do it when my family did not help clean? I was lucky that no one had come to view the property. I thought maybe I might be able to set to that week, not that day though. For the rest of the day I watched TV, and slept. As arranged the counsellor came to see me, a different one. She made the same comments, asked about the relationship between Max and I and said how lucky I was that he supported me financially. But I was concerned about the amount I would owe him when the house was eventually sold.

I had various counsellors visit during the week. They talked about debt management, suggested I go to the council as there was a debt management team that would be able to give me help. One counsellor asked about my finding employment. That was a big issue, what could I do? I remember one lady said that I did not know what was out there for me, and I remember making a note to get the local paper. That same week, I had to meet with Dr Chawla! I was escorted by a psychiatric nurse. I was embarrassed and ashamed. I felt I had let him down. What would he say to me? In the consultant's room, Dr Chawla started talking to the nurse about the time I had had a relationship with Angus, the fireman. I could not understand why he did, particularly how I handled the break-up, contacting his wife. I could not see what that had to do with my situation now. Once he had established that I had discussed my problems with the counsellors and psychiatric nurses and he had got reassurance from me that I would take my olanzapine again, he was happy to see me in two months' time.

I spent the rest of that year smoking and drinking, staying in bed, not communicating with anyone but Max. I still continued to see him twice a week, but he had no idea of the amount I smoked or drank. No one came to view the house. I felt that I would review it after Christmas. I did, however, go to the debt management team at the council offices, but as I would be solvent once the house was sold, they could not help me, I was just to wait until the house was sold.

Christmas came; I spent it at Max's, my daughter again spent it at her fiancé's parents' and my son with friends. I thought it would be a break for them, seeing me in such a state must have been upsetting. A whole Christmas without smoking, the occasional drink seemed to get me more focused. Being away from home, I was able to view my situation. Back home, the New Year! I didn't go back to smoking. I somehow did not need it; my family was impressed. I knew that I needed to look at getting a new job, not sure what, but I was ready to start looking.

Chapter Twenty-One

I spent the first few months of the new year looking for a new job. I was becoming more positive; also, helping my daughter with her wedding plans, scheduled for the following September, helped me. My financial input for the wedding was all based on when I sold the house. I did, however, feel that I would like to pay for the wedding dress. I had gone with her to choose it and she looked beautiful. The plans were coming together, the venue chosen, I was getting excited. Somehow I could see my daughter getting married from the house. With the economy being what it was, I had reduced the price, but still with no firm offers.

Whilst looking for a job, I had started to look for a position in care. I read with interest in the local newspaper a vacancy for a support worker. It was to assist people with autism and learning difficulties. It said no experience was necessary. I was just taking down the telephone contact number when I received a text from my son. It said that I was going to become a grandmother in June of that year! I was shocked, I had no idea that the relationship had developed so far. Also how could he send a text, could he not tell me face to face? I assumed that the young lady in question was the person I had met, on occasion in passing, at home. I sent a text back saying 'I think we need to talk' – how had he kept this from me, the young lady in question must be four/five months into her pregnancy!

Talking to him that evening, I established that he had found out about the pregnancy on the day I had attempted to take my life and it wasn't planned. What a Friday the thirteenth! He had kept it from me as I was not in a good state of mind. He planned to move in with his girlfriend, Sue, whom I had met on occasion. Becoming a grandmother – I was not ready, I somehow did not seem old enough. Still, I would give them as much support as I could. I would very much like to meet with Sue, perhaps dinner with her would be appropriate. Diary note to set plans in motion.

I managed to get an interview with the local company as a support worker. I was quite excited at the prospect of finally getting a job. Max was still giving me £500 per week; so cash flow was acceptable to the bank manager. If only I could sell the house.

The interview went well, I found the company to be very professional and I waited eagerly for response from them; I would be very happy to accept the position if it was offered. A week later I got a telephone call from them to say that I was offered a second interview, this time with the residents I would be looking after. Apparently it would be up to them, they would have the final say on who would be employed. My luck was in, the residents took to me and I was offered the job there and then. I was to start in May, once my CRB had come through.

I was beginning to feel a lot better. Max had planned a holiday to France and Belgium by coach, scheduled for July, and my employers honoured it, so life was getting back on track. I finally started my employment, first in the main home for a few weeks. Coping with clients who had autism was quite gruelling, but I soon managed to cope and the management seemed happy with my progress. I then moved to supported living premises where the clients were not so tasking. I enjoyed this type of work better. It was at this time I met up with the proprietor as he spent time at my place of work. His name was Nigel. He had a degree in psychology and a very pleasing personality. We hit it off immediately and he very much appreciated my professional approach and caring manner. Before I would have been reluctant to talk with the owner, I would have felt that I was beneath him and not able to talk to an educated man. Psychology...I would not have understood what he was talking about, but now I could understand and make relevant comments to move the conversation on and also reflect on what each of us was saying and establish why we were like we were. This meant that we very much appreciated time spent with each other. How I had changed, it was as if I were able to listen, understand and return comments – nothing was holding me back. I also was able to feel comfortable with men. I somehow had finally got over the fear of them!

Chapter Twenty-Two

I had spent some time with Sue. She had come over for dinner, and we had discussed the birth of my grandchild. She said that she wanted me to have an active part in bringing her child up. I did not feel comfortable with that, as I had just finished bringing my own children up; with my mental illness to cope with as well, I needed time to adjust. I did not, of course, tell her about this, I would wait to see how I felt when the baby arrived.

June came round quickly. My son had moved out of my dwelling and all was ready for the birth of my grandchild.

The day arrived – my first grandchild was born: a baby girl. I did not go to the hospital, but waited until Sue and baby were home. My son had been present at the birth, and was very attentive to the cutest little girl who was resting in his arms when I arrived at their home. She had blonde hair and the most beautiful blue eyes. My son seemed to have changed. He was calmer, and so proud of his daughter. My uneasiness at becoming a grandmother faded, and I too was so proud to nurse his child. I did not stay long, but said I would make regular visits if that was suitable to the proud parents.

Max and I went to France and Belgium on a coach holiday. I really enjoyed the trip by coach. We spent time in the shops, buying the cutest dresses for my granddaughter. It lasted just four days but it gave me time to reflect on my new job, becoming a grandma and the wedding, pending in September that year. Still no buyer for my property, so it looked as if my daughter would be leaving from home – what a relief. There would be enough room for her to have the bridesmaids get ready there the morning of the wedding.

Coming home, Max and I spent time together as normal, twice weekly, but I was not convinced that we were that close any more. Was it the job taking a lot of my time, being a grandma or arranging the wedding for my daughter? Not sure. The £500 per week was still going into my bank account, less what I received from my employment. I dreaded to think what I would owe him when I finally moved out.

Due to the turmoil of the past years, my mum was the only one of my family coming to the wedding apart from my immediate family. She arrived the day before the wedding. I was very stressed, as she still reminded me of the past, of when I was a child; that had definitely not gone away. Her mannerisms brought back to me the time when I was so vulnerable, and worry about the house sale and the wedding plans did not make me feel well at all. I could definitely say I was not looking forward to the wedding.

The wedding morning was sunny. There was a relay for showers, hairdressers, make-up. Max arrived early and prepared a lovely wedding breakfast with champagne. All was going well as long as I did not spend much time with my mum. She was so loud! I found it difficult to express my feelings and help prepare everyone for this memorable day. It was time to go to the venue. I relaxed when I saw my daughter ready in her attire, like a princess holding onto the arm of my son, who was giving her away. I was so proud of them both, I fought back tears over the memories of bringing them up, what lay ahead with my financial concerns, and Max, what was happening to us.

The day went off well. One of the proudest moments was seeing my children walk down the aisle, laughing and looking so happy. The wedding ceremony went well, the meal and speeches and flow of champagne put everyone in a jovial mood and many danced well into the evening. Unlike at previous wedding ceremonies Max and I did not seem to enjoy the dancing and socialising with other guests. I was not feeling as happy in his company as I had on previous occasions. Was the pressure getting too much for us both?

Back at work, normality. At home, I had a viewing! And they put in an offer. It was not what I expected, but I took it on board, spoke to Max that evening, slept on it and decided to accept the offer! They wanted a quick sale, no chain. But things never run smoothly. Initially, they found damp and that the roof needed attention so we had to negotiate a reduction; later we established there was no building regulations for the alterations made before I purchased the property, so I had to fork out £1,800 to get the council to come and do a structural survey, only to find that the doors would have to be replaced with fire doors, alarms on each floor! How can I explain how I felt? Would there be anything left after the sale? How I managed to keep sane and work plus cope with all the pressure of the sale was remarkable. Christmas of 2010 came, I had started packing; it came and went. In addition, my son's relationship had broken up and he had moved back in. That was an additional concern. I somehow managed to sort the furniture out that my son needed for a flat and what I would take to Max's home. The rest went to the tip courtesy of a removal firm. I had a few days off work to arrange all this and the move finally happened in February 2011!

I did the house clearance myself, no one to help me. When I arrived at Max's with my few sticks of furniture and suitcases I was incredibly shattered. I had smoked cigarettes for the last few months, and now moving into Max's I had to stop. I sat in the lounge waiting for him to come home. His house was a palace, he did not have a thing out of place, not even a cushion. How was I going to cope with his fastidiousness?

How do I explain the next few weeks? We did not argue, but we were very quiet. Max was still thinking he was alone – he did the shopping himself, did the housework, the washing, I was the lodger. I dreaded the time spent with him. Going to bed early not wanting to spend time with him helped, but we never stopped having sex! After three weeks, he came home from work and after dinner he announced that he wanted me to move out!! I was shocked, I could not believe that after all this time he wanted me to go. He said he didn't know if he still loved me or not. How could he have let me get rid of my furniture and then say he wanted me out? I ran upstairs, leaped into bed trying to absorb what he had just told me. When a voice in my head said 'This is what you wanted'! Max came into my bedroom at that point and asked me if I was all right. I replied, 'Yes' and suggested we have a drink to start planning things in order for me to move out. He could not believe my approach to this dilemma and agreed. We had a drink and started to sort things out. How I accepted this trauma with such calmness I shall never know; however, the days and weeks leading to the day I moved out were intolerable. When I wasn't at work I drank, buying a bottle of wine at a local shop then sitting in a lay-by in the car drinking the entire bottle and smoking ten to fifteen cigarettes before going home. Once at home I managed to cook a meal, hiding my intoxication from Max when he came home. I at times tried to persuade him to change his mind but he still kept saying no. In a way I was glad, but I was anxious about living on my own. A couple of weeks before I moved into a flat I had arranged to rent, Max took me to the town to buy me everything I needed for the flat, from a washing machine to a CD player. All I had to buy was bed linen and kitchen utensils. Was this guilt? He had talked about still keeping in touch. Was this why he had made the flat comfortable? We were still having sex!!?

The day of my move came. I was stressed and anxious. Once everything was in my flat I had to say goodbye to Max. I did not cry, and in a way I was glad. After leaving him at the doorstep, I went upstairs, lit a cigarette and had a glass of wine. The next week was fantastic, I had a week off work to get sorted. I had no one to answer to. No children, no man, just me. For the first three days I smoked and drank to excess! Then I decided enough was enough. I wanted to give up smoking, reduce drinking and go on a diet. I could not believe the changes in me. Max had telephoned me in the week with a view to coming round to see me, but I declined the offer. He was amazed to hear that I had stopped smoking, reduced the drink and gone on a diet. He could not believe the changes in me, he thought I would have done the opposite. Was I proud of myself?

After sorting my finances, paying back my debts, I had about £25,000 to invest for my retirement. I did a budget for my costs in the flat and what I had left to spend. Having money left was something I had not been used to for a long time. Max came round for a drink and a meal out during the summer of 2011. I enjoyed the time spent with him and he was shocked how I had changed, so positive about the future, looking better for the weight loss, reduced drinking and no smoking. He said I was thriving and was like a magnet; I believe he said I was so attractive and sexy. Gosh, I was fifty-nine and still having sex! If anything I enjoyed talking with him about my progress. I had such inspirations about the future.

It was at this time that I went on a holiday with Nigel and two residents to Center Parcs. I knew if I was to spend time with Nigel I would disclose my childhood experiences to him. It started when we were driving down to the Parc. He was shocked that I had overcome such trauma and was such a remarkable woman. He was so excited about my future. He said I had such a lot to offer the world. He said, using his psychology terms, that I was on a plateau with seeds already set for the future. I was sound, recovered, already helping others and I was not to worry about the future. Dr Chawla had only recently said that I had overcome my problems and he did not want to see me any more, but I should still, however, take my olanzapine daily. Nigel's comments confirmed my suspicions that I had a lot to offer the world and my need to help those who had had the same experiences was paramount. I had already started to talk to a member of staff at work who had had similar experiences, which I found gratifying. Nigel did not know how much his words meant to me.

I came home after the holiday with Nigel refreshed and inspired. Whatever possessed me I shall never know, but I found myself driving to my local college and once there asking about courses in counselling! I had never been to college and did not know if they would take me on at the age of fifty-nine. I found to my delight there was a course starting in January the next year. I arranged a meeting with the course tutor and to my surprise she accepted me. It was a four-year course and I explained that at the end of the course I wanted to counsel young adults who had been sexually abused. I should have a diploma once I had completed the entire four years. I now realised that I had overcome my ordeals from my young life and thanks to Dr Chawla my life would be completely different from now on.........